M000114512

UNDER THE

X

IN TEXAS

UNDER THE

X

IN TEXAS

Little Stories from the Big Country

Mike Renfro

─────────────

Texas Tech University Press

© Copyright 1995 Texas Tech University Press

All rights reserved. No portion of this book may be reproduced in any form or by any means, including electronic storage and retrieval systems, except by explicit, prior written permission of the publisher, except for brief passages excerpted for review and critical purposes.

This book was set in Cheltenham and Copperplate and printed on acid-free paper that meets the guidelines for permanence and durability of the Committee on Production Guidelines for Book Longevity of the Council on Library Resources. ∞

Lyrics from "The Front Porch Song" by Robert Earl Keen, Jr., and Lyle Lovett, copyright 1984 Keen Edge Music, and from "Under the 'X' in Texas" words and music by Johnny Gimble, copyright 1975 Gardenia Music, BMI, are reprinted with permission.

Text and jacket design by RBMM, Dallas

Cover photos by Jim Olvera

Manufactured in the United States of America.

Library of Congress Cataloging-in-Publication Data
Renfro, Mike.
        Under the X in Texas : little stories from the Big Country / Mike Renfro.
        p.   cm.
        ISBN 0-89672-355-0 (alk. paper)
        1. Texas—Social life and customs—Anecdotes. I. Title.
F391.2.R46 1995
976.4—dc20   95-32155
                                                              CIP

96 97 98 99 00 01 02 03 04 / 9 8 7 6 5 4 3 2

Texas Tech University Press
P. O. Box 41037
Lubbock, TX 79409-1037 USA
1-800-832-4042

To Brenda, endurer of countless idiosyncracies, dumb jokes, and my not entirely cured red neck. Your love and understanding made that which follows flow more freely.

To Brack Bledsoe, my eighth-grade speech teacher, whose influence on my life confirms that we pay our athletes too much, and our teachers, not nearly enough.

And to Baxter Black, who sent my first essay to National Public Radio, and paid me the ultimate compliment in saying that I write like he talks.

ACKNOWLEDGMENTS

Much of what is written here originally appeared in recorded form on National Public Radio's "Weekend Edition Sunday" and "Morning Edition," from August 1992 through November 1994. My thanks to NPR producers Mark Schramm, Bob Muleski, and Greg Smith for your support and encouragement.

So, I get this call back in '91. It's The Richards Group ad agency, which I'd never heard of, but ad agencies seem to have the longevity of a tanning salon. Mike Renfro introduces himself and asked if I'd be interested in making radio commercials for the State Fair of Texas.

I said maybe. Except . . . I don't use my name, I don't do jingles, I don't sign contracts and we do 'em at my house. He mused through my requests and asked, "Do you have a studio?" I told him I did and that's where I made my NPR commentaries. He said he had no problem with that. That's how he worked with Tom Bodett to make the motel commercials. He had picked me out from hearin' me on NPR.

I assumed he would send me the information and I would write the commercials. But no, he said he would write them. I admit I worried a little because when you talk funny and have an odd accent it's hard to read commercials written with Robin Leach or Wolfman Jack in mind.

Anyway, Mike showed up on the appointed date and brought the radio copy. To my surprise, they were easy for me to read. I asked him how he did it. He said he listened to my cowboy poetry cassettes for days — then wrote 'em! I was impressed. He was able to write like I talked! And I thought I was the only one.

His stories that I hear on NPR's Weekend Edition are a trip to the soft spot in your heart. Though I don't call myself a Texan, I did live in Lubbock as a grade schooler before movin' west. Mike's commentaries are like Grandma explainin' the old photos in her shoebox. I know the people, the places, the heat, the black top road and the old fashioned way some folks still are.

It's the same feelin' I got when I saw the movie, "Hud." I recognized the flat dusty country and the people who lived in those hard west Texas towns. "They got it right," I said. Even if Paul Newman didn't talk like a telephone operator from Midland.

Mike captures the essence of bein' a Texan. Just from goin' to grade school there I know what that is. Texas history is instilled in the kids. Whether you're a Mexican immigrant's kid from El Paso, a Jewish banker's kid from Dallas, a black cowboy's kid from Victoria, a German butcher's kid from Boerne or a gringo cotton farmer's kid from Patricia, you're taught to be proud of bein' a Texan. Every kid can sing the state song. Most kids elsewhere don't even know what their state song is. Texas makes Texans feel special.

I've been told to be a good writer, you should write about what you know. In Mike's case, he writes about what he cares for. It's hard to shed light on important things in life using great sweeping vistas that encompass sunrise in Tyler and sundown in Ft. Davis. Especially in a three-minute commentary. Mike chooses to write about geriatric drive-in theaters, old barbers, squeaky screen doors and things not spoken.

He is able to illuminate an ant hill along the freeway of life that gives some meaning to the fastlane in which we're trapped.

We're all headed in different directions, but Mike takes us home.

Baxter Black
Cowboy poet, former large animal veterinarian and irregular commentator on NPR's Morning Edition

CONTENTS

Modern-Day Things as Seen through Decidedly
   Unmodern Eyes

Under the

X

in Texas

I'm sittin' here lookin' at a map I got laid out on my lap.
There ain't too many places I ain't been.
But the one place I love best is spread all over the West.
And I'm tryin' to figure out how to get back home again.
I wish I was sittin' right under the "X" in Texas.
Right in the heart of where my heart must be.
No matter where I roam, I never feel at home, 'cept in Texas,
And under the "X" in Texas is where I'd like to be.

Johnny Gimble
"Under the 'X' in Texas"

WHAT IS IT WITH YOU PEOPLE, ANYWAY?

———————————

A lady in California with whom I worked posed this question to me when I told her I was returning to Texas after only eight months or so in Los Angeles. Seems I wasn't the first person she'd known from my state to do such a thing, and she made no secret that she failed to understand what made Texans feel so much different from other people.

"You're so damned parochial. You'd think there wasn't anyplace else in the world, to hear you talk about it," she went on. "Here you are, living in the most amazing place on earth, and you don't even appreciate it."

It was at that point I knew there was no common ground upon which we could continue the conversation, for while in some ways Los Angeles certainly was amazing, I had the nagging feeling that "amazing" was a word that could apply readily to certain qualities of Hell and angioplasty, as well.

Amazing, yes. Inviting, no.

Texas, for whatever reasons, is simply one of those places that fuels the imagination of many. Now, if you happen to find yourself stuck in line at a Wal-Mart in Grand Prairie, you may wonder why on earth that is. However, if you happen to be wandering along the banks of the Frio River in the Hill Country, or anywhere in the Big Bend, there certainly will be no question.

Point being, it's not one place, but a whole lot of different places, and before I start sounding like a tourist brochure, just suffice it to say there's beauty, ugliness, some of the finest people ever to set foot on this planet, and some of the most vile, disgusting scum to crawl out from under a Porta-Potty. Probably more of the latter than we'd like to admit.

Of course, you could say those things about a lot of places, but I think the difference here is one of extremes. The weather here is damned hot and damned cold. Sometimes both within the same day. Sometimes both within the same hour. Texas always has been and always will be a place of extremes, and for better or worse, it shows up in the souls it puts out. Like the weather, these people might not always make you feel comfortable, but each extreme makes you appreciate the other.

It certainly doesn't make for a great deal of mediocrity, anyway. How else does one explain a place that produces the likes of Roy Oribison, Buddy Holly, Jack Ruby, Admiral Nimitz, Denton Cooley, Howard Hughes, Bonnie and Clyde, Elmer Wayne Henley, Don Henley (no relation), Janis Joplin, Scott Joplin (again, no relation), Spanky McFarlane, Carol Burnett, Lee Harvey Oswald, and a ton of others— good, evil, eccentric, and sometimes all of the above.

Whatever it is, there is something different—if not special—about this place. I think it's special, but I'm biased. I live here. If you've never spent time in Texas (and I don't mean at DFW airport), maybe some of the stories herein will give you an idea why some of us are the way we are. Not trying to justify anything, you understand, just show us for what we are.

Some of the tales that follow are nothing more than observations, but they are observations intended to frame the window many of us here see you through. This is a loose collection of stories, one not necessarily related to the other, but all under one cover nonetheless, much like a Texan from Diboll might have little in common with a Texan from Dumas, other than they are both Texans, which in most cases is enough.

If, by chance, you do live in Texas and still do not understand what all the fuss is about, I heartily recommend leaving the state for a time, then looking back upon what you have left and comparing it to the new place in which you reside. It is only then that you may see what a truly special and different place Texas is. This was my experience, anyway. And it confirmed for me that, like the love of one's parents, the full extent of what Texas is, often is not appreciated until viewed from outside its embrace.

This can be the only reasonable explanation why so many leave here only to return, and why so many others who don't return, never seem to get this place fully washed out of them, in spite of it all.

Mike Renfro
November 1994
Somewhere under the X

THIS PART OF

THE WORLD,

BEING WHAT IT IS

AND ALL

———————————

This old porch is The Palace walk-in on a main street in Texas.
It ain't never seen nor heard the days of "G" and "R" and "X-es."
With that '62 poster that's almost faded down.
And a screen without a picture since Giant came to town.

Robert Earl Keen, Jr., and Lyle Lovett
"The Front Porch Song"

WHERE THE STICKY THINGS START

——————————

I f you're not looking for it, the exact place will probably elude you. And most people, whizzing by as they do at seventy miles or more per hour, show greater concern for who's in front of them and what the kids are doing in the back seat than where it all begins.

There's no marker there, but I know where it is.

If you're traveling on the interstate, it's just a couple miles after you pass under Fort Worth's west side loop and leave the mini-mall and assorted car lot pandemonium behind. It's there, where only a couple of strip bars and beer joints have been relegated, that the careful observer can find its beginnings.

Post oak trees suddenly take their leave from around the edge of the road and the vista grows wide on both sides. The westerly view now gives hints of distant mesas in hazy blue. Gentle rolling of the land as you've passed out of town now grows more urgent, and a ledge on the right tells the rest.

Gnarled little yuccas begin to poke out of the rocks with their stems headed up toward some place undetermined, their spiny leaves waiting to give a painful reminder to any roadside wanderer exactly where it is they now find themselves.

It, as the post cards and Chamber of Commerce-types would say, is the place where the West begins. The spot at which the land starts to grow dryer and more hostile. Something that it will continue to do from this exact point all the way to the edge of the L.A. basin.

I know this spot as the place where the sticky things start. Those sticky things being the aforementioned yuccas, as well as prickly pear cactus, not to mention accompanying scorpions, tarantulas, and snakes found just as abundantly—and no less sticky, when improperly crossed.

To say the land here grows more unfriendly to casual intrusion is understatement to the extreme, but that unfriendliness makes it all the more worthwhile for the serious and dedicated explorer. It's a self-selecting place that weeds out the many and thus offers greater solace for the few.

More importantly, it is *my* place. If not on paper, then in my head and my heart, which I would suppose makes me a member of that few.

We are not, however, an overtly exclusive group by any means. Eccentric might even be a more proper word for the affliction. And an affliction it most certainly is in the eyes of our wives, friends, and assorted well-meaning relatives.

Most of them are lovers of the greener, wetter lands of great, tall pines and easily broken soils. To them, this place of mine is the beginning of waste, and a love for it, an exercise in folly.

So much the better, say I. And a fair-sized group of others would nod in agreement.

For if the price paid for a love of this place is the whispering and chuckling of others, then so be it. Most of the people here care little about those things, anyway. And the mere fact they choose to come here, either full- or part-time, is more than proof of it.

Charles Goodnight no doubt got more than an earful of the same whispering and chuckling when he cast his lot out in the middle of it all, at a time when it was far more inhospitable than now. Most likely he found the sound of the wind and the brutishness of the heat and thunderstorms far preferable to human clamor, anyhow.

And thus it is with me. And a few others. But not so many as to make it unappealing.

Hardheadedness and disdain of popular opinion can actually serve you pretty well here. Certainly a whole lot better than they ever will in the coat-and-tie, two cars and a swimming pool parts of this planet.

I know, because I've lived in that world—and live in it still a good deal of the time. Yet, it always has been the place where the sticky things start that I feel the grip of that other place loosen.

I can't say for sure why that is. Maybe those demons from that other world somehow sense their uselessness and scatter back to the east, leaving in their wake only the casualties of tossed-off neckties hanging from the pointy ends of the yuccas. Some of mine are among them.

The place where the sticky things starts has a way of stripping off the unnecessary and forcing you to take with you only that which is really needed. Call it God's own metal detector, if you will. Just avoid going through it with too much mental jewelry on.

If you follow that little ground rule, you'll very likely arrive at the place where I always eventually find myself: a patch of land more or less to the west by a little bit north of Mineral Wells on the edge of the Palo Pinto mountains.

To be truthful, it's a place well beyond where the sticky things start, and, in fact, a place where the sticky things have become quite well-established, thank you. Some fifty miles or so west of Fort Worth is a place where juniper-covered mesas rise out of the red rock up into the kick-butt sun, a place into which I can step as easily as I would an old pair of Wrangler jeans.

Why, I honestly cannot tell you. I guess that's because the essence of this place is not one single thing, but a whole bunch of different things all jumbled up into one roadside junk store of feelings and scenery.

The land is certainly a big part of it. In fact, I suppose if you asked someone what Texas is supposed to look like, this is what would come to mind. Cactus, rocks, cattle, rattlesnakes, pump jacks, mesquite trees, more cactus, more mesquite trees, and more rattlesnakes.

And then there are the people who step carefully, and thus manage to live among all that.

They're an interesting lot, to say the least. A substantial number of them are older, since this tends to be the kind of place younger people get out of in search of excitement. Then, of course, there's the smattering of people like me who come here having had all they can stomach of said excitement.

But mostly, it's older people. Those who've stayed the duration in this part of the world, and seem likely to stay until somebody lays them back into it. Good Christian ladies with white hair and incredible cooking skills. Old ranchers whose love of chewing tobacco has outlasted their teeth.

They'll be quick to tell you how sorry the land around here is, but only spit disgustedly and look off into the distance when asked why they never left.

There are a few longhaired types, who you'd think were bikers, to look at them. But their appearances belie their outlooks, which place them squarely in the same lot as the older people, as any brief conversation with them will confirm.

They've heard of political correctness only because Rush Limbaugh talks about it on the radio. Ask for the non-smoking section in a restaurant and you'll likely as not be shown to the parking lot.

I like that in a place.

Especially in these times of Big Brother telling us more and more what it is we should and shouldn't do. You do pretty much what you want to do here, as long as it doesn't bother anybody else. And if it does, you'll likely as not have a pistol waved in your face to draw attention to your error.

Some, most notably the Big Brother types, would surely frown on such things, but it's a system that's always worked around here. A quick check of the crime rate and a look at the lack of graffiti and decay around here will confirm that fact. So, if it ain't broke . . . well, you know the rest.

The towns, beyond the largest of Mineral Wells and the county seat/non-metropolis of Palo Pinto, are little more than wide spots in the road. Places like Graford, Mingus, Santo, Brad, and Gordon.

There are interestingly named peaks like Shut-in, School-house, and Antelope. Additionally, each bend of the clear-flowing Brazos river has it's own name. There's Flint, Garland, Fortune, B.C. Harris, Dog, and Bath bends. Each a story unto itself.

Even the large reservoir at the northwest corner of the county has a name with a certain quaintness—Possum Kingdom Lake.

In the middle of it lies Hell's Gate, where two large cliffs rise from either side of the water, offering a high-dive challenge to many a drunk or terminally-stupid recreator.

Possum Kingdom, with it's cliffs and deep blue water, is really the only place here that's brought much influx of those from the outside. High-dollar places along the shores of the lake offer testament to that. But mostly those people make a beeline from their homes back in Dallas or Fort Worth to their weekend places here, and take little notice of that which is in between.

So, the rest of the place is pretty much left to me. And the ones who were already here. No influx of crystal-clanging New Agers or sixties dropouts has yet struck this part of the world as it has in some parts of the Texas Hill Country and Big Bend. Of course, I suppose that's always a possibility, but somehow I suspect it's not much of a worry. Thus, the land prices remain lower than a rancher's opinion of a P.E.T.A. convention, and the occasional opportunist like myself can manage to get a piece of it.

You won't find it listed on any map, as such, but I call my little piece of it Mike's Mesa. Fully half of it is just that, with a view west, east, and south, just begging for a house from which to look out on it all. For now, there's only a little stone place, down in the valley. Nothing fancy, but enough to keep the rain out.

For my part, I come out on weekends, tethered as I am during the week to the office from which the money flows. And I hold out hope that someday soon the fax machine and computer will allow me to ply my trade full-time from here.

It could certainly be argued with some success that it is a frivolous expense, this piece of unwelcoming, unforgiving land. What with a kid on the way and future college expenses being what they're projected to be, the left brain frequently yells at the right side for its foolishness. But then the right side has pretty much always ruled the roost inside this particular cranium, and the prospects of that changing seem dim at best.

Truth be told, I'm just another in a long line of people who've allowed this place and the thorny little things that populate it get under their skin.

Reason thus goes out the window like a Coors can out of a speeding truck, left there for somebody else to pick up. Besides, when it gets right down to it, walking the financial straight and narrow doesn't offer much opportunity for interesting detours. Certainly not into this kind of place.

That's a sad thing.

Regardless of all the going against the grain this place requires, I'm better for visiting here. And I hold some measure of faith that the soon-to-be kid, or kids, will reap the same benefits. As for college, that'll happen somehow or another.

Besides, in the grand scheme of things, there's at least as much here to be learned as in any classroom where I've ever done time. But like the classroom, you have to pay attention to this place to get anything out of it.

I'm one of those who do. And I will continue to do so.

Of course, inevitably, I have to go back to the east, towards work, and thus leave behind, however temporarily, the place where the sticky things start. And with each trip back, I find that sticky things of a more urban and insidious nature creep back into my head, making it clear why I came out here in the first place, and thus setting off a mental countdown, whose time will pass far too slowly.

At least, that is, until I'm back out here again.

The ghosts of Dealey Plaza in Dallas most often are outnumbered by the people who come in search of them. Especially as November 22 grows near.

Most afternoons, the plaza is filled by an odd assortment of the curious, the video enthusiasts, and those just there to look and listen.

It is with those listeners whom I've always felt the greatest kinship. They come not so much to gawk, as to think. I've found the best time for this contemplation is in the moments around sunrise.

And if, as it does every few years, the twenty-second falls on a Sunday, so much the better. To come to this place and listen to what its silence has to say in the peace of a Sunday morning is by far more moving than at any other time. There's no traffic to drown out the emotion that still hangs very heavy here. Without the endless parade of Hondas and Toyotas and busses down Elm Street, you can glance across at the Texas School Book Depository and pretend it's thirty-some-odd years ago.

I sat, on this particular morning, in the dewy grass next to the sidewalk and looked up at that window.

The window.

I longed for it to somehow gain a voice, to tell me its story. On reflection, I decided even if such a thing were to occur, the voice would simply say the story was far too sad to tell and request only that I leave it alone.

I shifted my gaze to the grassy knoll. That object of so much speculation over the years once again pleaded the fifth, leaving me, like Oliver Stone, to construct my own damned theory.

No, the walls around Dealey Plaza don't talk. But the echoes are just as loud as they ever were.

U nsettling is the word that first comes to mind.

Unsettling in the way it makes its appearance out of nowhere like an intruder standing over your bed, shocking you into consciousness but giving you no time to respond.

The rancher and the pipeline worker know the feeling well, but find no solace in its familiarity.

A sweaty day of plowing or soldering gives rise to a wiping of the brow and a casual glance up at the western horizon. The inevitable gape-eyed double take that follows confirms it. The sky suddenly looks pregnant with a weird greenish-blackness that hangs down like dirty rock-wool insulation through a rotted-out ceiling.

Thunder rumbles off in the distance. The air becomes unnervingly still. New spring leaves on mesquite trees turn a strange shade of bright green. And the normal mid-afternoon racket of unseen creatures seems to take on an urgent tone. They know what's coming.

If this is not enough to get your attention, the quiet of the land tells the tale. That is, if you know how to listen.

Fat cows huddle together in rocky pastures along the side of the road. Birds soar on the shifting breezes and get in one last quick flight for food. They seem to know, too.

Loud blasts of static electricity pop and buzz over country and western songs that play on old AM radios.

Ranchers' wives take down their brooms and clear cob webs from around storm cellar doors. Old men take note of which joints hurt, compare their pains to previous comings of storms, and try to guess how bad it'll get.

Mobile home owners, for the four-hundred-fifty-third time, curse their choice of dwelling and vow to dig a hole in the ground before the next one comes.

But for now, future-tense holes are of no service to their would-be diggers, and a bit of good luck is the best that can be hoped for.

The thunderstorm womb has birthed another problem child and the whole of the Big Country will feel the sting of its tantrums.

It starts out in the rough terrain and runs more or less in a line from Wichita Falls down west of Abilene, then less certainly to San Angelo. The thunderstorm womb's not on any map, but I know it's there. The old men's joints know it too.

It's not a place on the ground per se. Nor is it a place in the sky. It is a part of both, however. A feature that dwells in that fourth-dimensional Bermuda triangle kind of place, somewhere out there. A force never really seen, but demanding to be reckoned with nonetheless.

Meteorological types no doubt have some sort of explanation for the thunderstorm womb and why it is where it is. And I suspect their explanation would condemn it as little more than a folkloric place existing only in the heads of people who are given to too much contemplation of the things around them. People like me, in other words.

That the spring thunderstorm lines all seem to come from there could be written off as mere coincidence. Nothing more than the random result of where moist air blown up from the gulf happens to have its head-on collision with the equally determined and headstrong cold air out of the north.

Maybe so.

I certainly make no claim to have the numbers and charts and graphs to take serious issue with such an explanation. But then again, I care little for any such business. I like my own explanations. And what's more, I like the hurting joint theories of the old men who believe little of anything that doesn't originate with them or those equally as old and crotchety as themselves.

To them, the thunderstorm womb is as real as the liver spots on their hands and the laugh-line wrinkles in their faces. And so it is for me, as well.

Comanche descendants might surmise that it's there as a curse from God on the people who took the land from their ancestors. And I suppose a good case could be made for this theory. It's just possible that the spirits of long-dead warriors rise up out of the rocks and gullies and boil up into a frenzy in the afternoon heat. A close encounter with one of the more ornery storms might give you cause to believe all that. Especially as hail the size of Ruby Red grapefruit beats your pickup like a cheap drum, with no overpasses for miles. And if there was an overpass, you couldn't see it, because 2:00 p.m. has turned darker than Halloween night, causing that mortgage life insurance policy you took out last month to creep up from the back of your mind right into the front. There it makes itself right at home next to the thoughts you now have about who'll show up when they put you in the ground, and whether you ever paid back that forty bucks you borrowed from your best friend a few weeks ago.

The thunderstorm womb can make you think like that.

And who knows? Maybe it is old Comanches getting back their pound of flesh. The ferocity of it all is certainly something they'd be proud of. And even if it's not, it's still fun to impart the theory to the uninitiated and see the strange and pitying looks you get back when you've said it.

For my part, I tend to think that the womb's the result of the battle between east and west, north and south. A struggle between cultures and environments that plays out its battles regularly in the same place.

Kinda like Mother Nature's own World Wrestling Federation Championship Tag-Team Death Match. Only here, the winners and losers haven't been predetermined. Thus, it can be a lot more interesting.

It certainly makes sense that such a battle would take place in this part of the world. After all, the same types of struggles have been ripping at this place ever since it was a place. At various times, it's been Mexicans against Anglos, cattlemen against farmers, urban against rural, Catholic against Baptist, Baptist against Baptist, and do-gooders against leave-me-aloners. If the irresistible force is going to meet the immovable object, likely as not, they'll meet in Texas.

The struggles continue on the ground in this rough part of the world between San Angelo, Abilene, and Wichita Falls, and the struggle goes on too, in the sky up above it.

This place has always been a place of conflict and nastiness of one sort or another. The weather just continues the time-honored tradition.

And though it's not readily explainable in a purely scientific way, there is a long, crescent-shaped, but unseen thing, that really does run through the middle of my part of the world, and it is there that our springtime episodes of violence get their start.

If you still don't believe me, just wait and see.

For now, eyes in places like Rising Star and Ranger, Palo Pinto and Jacksboro look west and wonder how far away.

Preparations are made before the green boiling rolls in.

Rusted sheet metal clangs a warning against empty buildings in old forgotten business districts.

Tonight, tornadoes will dance in even the strictest of towns.

Form your own theory of why it is there. Just suffice it to say that the thunderstorm womb really is a place. Just as real as any volcano or fault line.

Confirmation of that fact is on its way just now.

And in the thick afternoon air, even those who doubt its fertility watch the sky and wait for their rebuke.

PAYING LAST RESPECTS TO THE WESTERNAIRE DRIVE-IN THEATER

Out a ways west of Fort Worth, where the number of real trees starts to dwindle in deference to mesquite and prickly pear cactus, there's an old, abandoned drive-in theater.

I'd passed by it for years, and like most on this highway, had given little thought to it. To this day, I still don't know what possessed me to steer the car down the overgrown gravel entrance on one oppressively hot afternoon last summer.

More than anything, I guess it was the faded painting on the back part of the screen that lured me in, much as it must surely have done during the days when people packed up the car with the kids and plenty of insect repellent for a John Wayne double-feature.

The painting, as best I could tell, was a cowboy hatted man and woman on horseback, looking as much as anything like a young Roy Rogers and Dale Evans. Despite the fact large portions of both their faces had weathered away, they continued smiling broadly. The man's right arm was raised and pointing at some unknown source of amusement off in the distance.

The name of the theater, now all but gone, was painted in a 1950s-style script just above their Stetsons in what looked to have once been red. It spelled out "Westernaire."

I stepped over a chain and walked by the forlorn ticket booth. The many-times broken magnetic marquee up above said "losed." The "c," much like the cars which had no doubt once flocked here, had long since disappeared.

It looked kind of funny in a way. In light of the deteriorated state of the Westernaire Drive-In Theater, the "closed" sign was a painfully obvious statement.

Making my way through the waist-high brush, I stepped carefully, wary of rattlesnakes that might have taken up residence in this seldom-visited place. The speaker stands stood in formation like little metal soldiers with nowhere to go. A few were bent over at varying angles. Still others were missing altogether.

A couple of the speakers, still attached to their wires, clanged against the poles, sounding a rhythmic dirge in the hot breeze. Large sections of the fabric that once covered the screen flapped in response.

Part of the snack bar had burned in the years since its glory days, and what was still standing didn't look as if it would do so for much longer. I opted against an attempted entrance and instead settled for a look through the broken window. A surprised armadillo scurried across the floor in alarm at my intrusion. The only truly identifiable thing in the place was a bulletin board labeled "Coming Attractions."

I decided to end my trespassing and let the corpse of the Westernaire Drive-In Theater rest in peace, resisting the temptation to grab one of the speakers on my way back out to the car.

The sign I passed as I walked out the exit now took on a pleading quality which I am certain was never intended by its authors.

It read, "Please Come Back."

I n the most basic of terms, a barber shop is to a hair stylist what a beat-up '68 GMC pickup truck is to a European sports car. Both are made for roughly the same purpose; the key difference is how they get you there.

This was the analogy that occurred to me just last Saturday as I made my first trip back to a regular barber shop in some years. Like many, I had bought into the curious early seventies' notion that a stylist was somehow better than the time-honored barber.

As I stepped inside, it appeared nothing had changed in twenty-five years—including the fashion preferences of the three men who plied their trade there.

There was a little chart on the wall to illustrate the various cuts available, just like the one in Floyd's Barber Shop on the *Andy Griffith Show*. There was the flat top, the crew cut, the standard men's cut. There were jars full of blue water, purpose unknown, and a sales display with foldable pocket combs offered at reasonable prices. Each barber's workspace was covered with the usual random scattering of scissors and clippers, both electric and non, and there were straight razors, and belts for sharpening of said razors.

Blow dryers were nowhere to be found.

This day, all three barber chairs were in use, each one turned slightly askew toward the twenty-four-inch TV screen at the end of the room. The patrons' heads were situated in such a way to make it possible for the barbers to work their magic while simultaneously watching *Bonanza*. In one of the barber shop's few concessions to the modern age, I noted that the set was indeed color.

In this establishment, pot luck was the order of the day, so whenever a chair emptied, you climbed in and took your chances. I got George, a big, hulking man with a beard and an economy of words.

He asked me how I'd like it cut, nodded, and went to work, returning a substantial part of his gaze to watching the travails of the Cartwright family.

By the time Hoss pulled Little Joe out of a fight, the haircut was done. I paid the man, threw in a dollar tip, and headed for the door. The next guy passed me on his way to George's chair, just in time for the beginning of *Maverick*, starring James Garner. He asked for a standard men's cut, tapered back. (The man, I mean, not James Garner.)

I walked outside and headed for the car. A beat-up old GMC pickup truck with no bumpers, squeaky shocks, and burned-out valves passed by on the street. I found the irony as

thick as the white smoke that blew from it's barely attached
tailpipe.

I began wondering how I was gonna break the bad news to
my hair stylist.

ASSORTED INANIMATE OBJECTS,

FARM ANIMALS, AND OTHER THINGS

WITH WHICH I'VE HAD

THE PLEASURE OF BECOMING ACQUAINTED

———————

This old porch is just a big old red and white Hereford bull
Standing under a mesquite tree in Agua Dulce, Texas.
He just keeps on playin' hide 'n' seek with that hot August sun.
He's sweatin' an' a pantin' 'cause his work is never done.

Robert Earl Keen, Jr., and Lyle Lovett
"The Front Porch Song"

TUESDAYS TO THE GROCERY STORE, FRIDAYS TO THE BEAUTY SHOP

The first thing you'll notice as you walk into my grandmother's house in the old part of Longview, Texas, is the 1960 Pontiac parked under the carport. Resting pretty much in the same place it has been since it was bought new from the Brew Pontiac Dealership in April of its model year, the great finned beast sits and waits. It's generally called into service just twice a week–Tuesdays, a trip to the Brookshire's store over on the loop for groceries, and Fridays, the beauty shop smack dab in the middle of what used to be downtown. The latter is one of those old-time beauty shops, where the customers sit under the big hairdryers and talk to the ladies next to them.

Parts of the Pontiac are beginning to rust now. Especially up on the hood that for so many years has sat beneath the incessant dripping of the old window air conditioner. Engine's fine, though.

I open the big white door on the driver's side, which is never locked, and am greeted by the strange plastic fragrance of vinyl seats that are older than I am. They are bench style, done in a strange blue color–an artificial blue, like the background the traveling photographer uses for taking baby pictures at K-Mart. A blue that does not and never has occurred naturally on this earth.

There are seat belts somewhere in the recesses of these seats, and I challenge you to find them.

Leaning into the steering wheel is one of those old fold-down seat cushions, somewhat popular during the 1960s. Probably purchased by my grandfather, it remains, some twenty years after his passing, every bit as defiantly out of style as the car in which it resides.

The radio is AM. The knob permanently turned to the "off" position, as "all that noise" makes my grandmother nervous. The clock, that never did keep good time, still doesn't. It continues ticking nonetheless. It reads 3:35.

Of course, it's not 3:35 in Longview, Texas. Maybe not in any time zone anywhere on earth. But in this car, it is.

The ashtray won't open. Maybe it never did. Anyway, it's never been used.

The glovebox falls open with a loud screech and a heavy thud. Inside is a yellowed owner's manual, a long-since useless warranty book, and an improperly folded 1967 Enco State of Texas map. What should be the map cover is now on the inside. It features the Humble Tiger and a neatly uniformed service station attendant leaning up against a gas pump, and offers a scripted wish for "Happy Motoring."

Underneath the map is a set of two keys whose purpose is uncertain. There are six pennies and a nickel, none dated later than 1964. They lie atop a couple of repair invoices upon which the handwriting is no longer visible. Underneath these is a blackened dime, unreadable and forever affixed by some mysterious gumlike substance to the bottom of the metal glove box.

Closing the box requires some measure of brutality, but after a couple of sharp blows strategically applied just below the latch, the door surrenders and remains shut.

Sitting back up straight behind the wheel, I look at the odometer. It stares back. 52,874. That's all. Thirty-two years of my grandmother's mainly Tuesday trips to the Brookshire's for groceries and Fridays to the beauty shop where you still sit under the hairdryer and talk to the ladies sitting next to you.

She turns ninety-two this summer, though, and finally had to give up driving.

So now the big white car sits patiently like an old dog, waiting for a master that won't be coming back.

I opened the big white door on the driver's side and climbed out. The old seat cushion fell back onto the steering wheel and the clock that never did work right continued to tick. It read 3:35.

Time stands still in my grandmother's Pontiac, and nowhere else.

A while back, I bought this piece of land out near West Texas, on the edge of what around here is known as The Big Country. It's a sparsely populated area of mesas, prickly pear cactus, a lot of cows, and the people who take care of them.

Most people don't know much about it, and that's one of the things that attracted me to it. It's a good place to get away from a world that seems more and more to want to tell you how to live your life.

A couple weeks ago, I took an out-of-state friend of mine to the place. For the most part, it was a pretty uneventful trip. Just us talking and catching up on old times as we drove along well above the posted speed.

I guess we were out around Millsap, or maybe near the town of Cool, when my friend asked me what it was I was doing.

"What do you mean?" I asked, not really knowing to what he was referring.

"What is that you always do with your index finger everytime a car or pickup passes by the other direction. You seem to kinda raise it up like you're pointing at them, or something."

"Oh that," I said, now having figured out the object of his curiosity. "That's the West Texas Wave."

"You know all those people?" he asked.

"Well, no," I responded.

"But you still wave at 'em," he said.

"Is roadkill colorful?" I shot back. "Of course I wave at 'em."

This was an amazing thing for my out-of-state friend to behold and consider. In his home state, you didn't wave at people in other cars you didn't know. In fact, the only way people passing on a highway there exchanged pleasantries was maybe by not shooting at one another.

I told him that, as best I could figure, the West Texas Wave was a holdover from fifty or sixty years ago. In this part of the world, you were generally happy on those rare occasions when you were lucky enough to see someone else on the road.

Actually, in the old days the West Texas Wave was probably more of a wave than it is now. Over the years, it's become more casual, evolving into little more than a slight raising of the index finger above the steering wheel while you continue on your merry way.

My out-of-state friend was intrigued and wanted to try it. Being a gracious host, I pulled the truck off the road, got out, and traded places with him so he could try his hand.

A while after we got going again, a pickup truck came into view up ahead. It was a white Chevy dooley, with horse trailer in tow. It looked promising for my friend's initiation into West

Texas Wavedom, so you can well imagine his disappointment when he received no response from the oncoming vehicle.

Clearly hurt by the blacktop rebuff he'd just received, I did what I could to console him.

"Maybe there'll be another car up here in a few miles and you can try it on them," I said. "And maybe this time, you might try using your index finger, instead of the middle one."

One of the first things people notice when they come to Texas is the number of pickup trucks in this part of the world. Growing up here, I guess I never thought much about it. That is, 'til a business client from Chicago pointed it out the other day as we drove in from the airport.

"What on earth," he asked, "do all these people need trucks for?"

And I guess you'd just have to chalk it up to a cultural thing—that is, if such a word as "cultural" can be applied to such an implement as a pickup truck.

I don't necessarily think we have more of a need to haul stuff. It's just, I guess, that people like to know they *can* haul stuff should the need ever arise. I mean, people are still big into cowboy boots here in spite of the obvious lack of necessity for them. I suppose this provides great peace of mind; should a sudden storm of cow excrement cross your path, you're certainly prepared.

And in light of the recent abundance of said excrement at the Dallas Cowboys' headquarters, I suppose insulating one's self from such things is a good precaution to take—but I digress.

I guess the thing about pickup trucks is they were the most logical replacement for the horse and wagon. And, in fact, for a lot of people here, their trucks take on personalities of their own over time, much like an animal does.

Some of them have names. "Old Paint" is the highly appropriate name of my dad's truck—at least that's the name of the body into which he's put four or five different engines and about a half a million miles. It's not like he can't afford a new one, but there's something to be said for the comfort of familiarity. You get used to the way the doors creak when you open them and that certain way you have to hit the dashboard to make both speakers on the stereo come in just right.

"Big Red" was the name a good friend of mine gave his '67 GMC. He'd kept it from the scrap heap a good deal longer than was probably advisable. Even so, when it came time to get rid of the thing, it was an emotional parting. He couldn't stand the thought of having to buy a new truck. Especially one that didn't have a rusted-through hole in the driver's side floorboard into which he could spit.

These and other stories I related to my Chicago friend as we made our way into town in my four-door sedan with power windows and no spit holes whatsoever. He remained baffled, still unable to understand the attraction of the vehicles.

About that time, as the traffic began backing up on the Stemmons Freeway, a beat-up, mid-seventies Chevy half-ton sporting an unidentifiable color and tar all over the sides, jumped the rather substantial curb and blazed its own trail across the field to wherever it had in mind to go. It was then that my out-of-state companion noted, with some enthusiasm, that on second thought, maybe a pickup truck might not be such a bad idea in Chicago.

CLAY HENRY, THE BEER-DRINKING GOAT AND MAYOR OF LAJITAS

———————

You don't just pass through Lajitas, Texas. Either you intended to go there in the first place or else you are terribly, hopelessly lost. Lying along the Rio Grande in the middle of the Chihuahan Desert, daily life there has little to do with anything going on anywhere else in the country. The rises and falls of the stock market and who the president might happen to be are irrelevant. The people who choose to live their lives in this place like it that way. They must, to stay, for while it is indeed beautiful, it is equally harsh and unfriendly to permanent residency.

Suffice it to say, there are no Cineplexes or shopping malls to capture the interest of those looking for recreation. And I suppose that would, to some extent, explain the rise of one of the town's main attractions–a goat named Clay Henry, with a legendary thirst for cold beer.

Goats, of course, are a breed disdained by many and have never been known for their discriminating pallettes, but Clay Henry's thirst for the hops topped even that of some of the more notable local human rogues. After a time, Clay Henry became a tourist destination of such note that the locals elected him mayor, through an electoral process as hazy as the look in his perpetually bloodshot eyes. His honor held forth in a metal pen next to the general store in Lajitas before an endless stream of pilgrims who bore gifts in recyclable aluminum cans, the majority of which, on any given day, lay spent in large shiny heaps around the perimeter of his pen.

Understandably, those of an animal rights persuasion might see the whole thing in a dim light, but facts would say that no harm ever came to the goat from his thirst or those who readily quenched it for him. In fact, the honorable Clay Henry, mayor of Lajitas, Texas, did fairly recently meet his end, not by cirrhosis of the liver, but at the hands of his own offspring. Seems Clay Henry and his son, Clay Henry, Jr., became embroiled in a battle over a young female, a row that proved fatal to the elder goat.

Thus it was that, at the ripe old age of twenty-two years, Clay Henry, Sr., was laid to rest. An official period of mourning followed—at least it was as official as anything ever gets in Lajitas, Texas.

For now, Clay Henry, Jr., carries on in the same pen with the same propensity for cold beer. I understand Coors Light is his favorite.

In the meantime, the mayor pro tem has assumed all official duties—she being a large black dog of questionable ancestry with a propensity for catching frisbees. Those attempting to court her favor should note that, unlike her predecessor, the new mayor does not like beer. From all reports, she prefers mixed drinks.

In Rememberance of a Squeaky Screen Door

I suppose over the last thirty or forty or more years, there
have been plenty of things to pass from this world that are
well-deserving of some measure of grief. Certain models of cars
or airplanes come to mind. Old Route 66 is another piece of
the recent past missed by some more sentimental types like
myself. However, one of the things I miss most is something
probably not at the forefront of most people's minds. I'm
talking about the screen door. Most particularly, the one
attached, more or less, to my grandmother's house.

I say that because it never did seem, in all the years of my
memory, to ever quite fit in the frame. And you had to give it
a pretty good tug to get the little metal latch to find its mark
in the hole that held it semi-firm to that frame. Or at least good
enough to keep most of the bugs out. The house it guarded
was a fairly large, white, clapboard affair with a big, rusty
porch swing and a large, sheetmetal warehouse for all my
grandfather's stuff out beside it.

Screen doors are not so much needed anymore, I suppose.
The ubiquitous humming of air conditioners reminds us there's
no longer the need to let the air flow in like there once was.

What I liked most about screen doors, especially the one at my grandmother's house, was the noise it made whenever it was opened or closed. A loud screech, followed by a heavy thud. To me, this ugly thing with peeling forest green paint and a couple of patches in the screen was better than an English butler at the doorway, announcing the entry of the latest guest to my grandma's.

If you had the time or the inclination, as I did at that very young age, you could pretty much guess who was coming in by the song of the screen door. A very short screech, followed by an almost sonic boom of a thud was a certain indication that one of my cousins had gained entry and caution should be immediately taken to keep from getting melvined or noogied by them.

A longer, much slower, more low-pitched screeching of the door, and the creaking protestations of wood, indicated the arrival of my rather large-bellied Uncle Harold. Generally, this sound was followed by some serious throat clearing, a disturbing noise which generally confirmed it was, in fact, him.

Two knocks on the frame, then the door opening without any time for an answer to those knocks, meant Gladys from down the street was there to visit and pull quarters out of our ears.

Over time, the singing of the screen door took on more of an infirmed quality to its tones, 'til at the end of its life it seemed to almost be screaming with the pain of some sort of wood-borne arthritis. Holes in the screen had gone from being patched to just having bits of newspaper stuck in them, and eventually it grew even harder to wrestle it into its frame.

The screen door had grown cranky and was at the end of its days. It was no longer even up to its duties as sentinel against the myriad East Texas insects who liked my grandma's house as much as I did. Still, I was surprised and just a little sad when I arrived at her door to find it gone. A new glass model with a pneumatic opening and closing mechanism now hissed at you as you entered or left. No longer could you tell who had come to call by the sound and length of the screeching. Uncle Harold's hiss sounded pretty much the same as anyone else's.

I don't suppose any argument could be made against the efficiency of the new door with its airtight seal, keeping the bugs out and the air-conditioning in. Still, I couldn't quit thinking about the squeaking, that almost daily soundtrack to my earlier life, and the strange quietness now that I could hear it no longer.

Silliness, I thought, to get all worked up about an object as inanimate as a beat-to-hell screen door with newspaper stuck through it to plug the holes. After all, screen doors, no matter how much character you imagine into them, are just screen doors. And things that fade out of vogue and out of style are just things and not one bit more than that.

I wondered if anyone ever notices what those, and other things, take with them when they leave us. Or if most people even care. Moreover, I came to the undeniable conclusion that I'm just one of those who do.

———————————

M y grandmother says it's kind of weird being as old as she is.

"When you get to be old like me, everybody you knew coming up is pretty much gone now," she says.

"Either they've passed on literally or their mind has left their body behind on this earth."

But my grandmother is still here, both in mind *and* body, creaky and occasionally troublesome as it may be. As of a few weeks ago, she is the same age as the century in which we currently find ourselves, though it seems to me she's weathered things much better than this world has.

Americans generally don't pay much attention to people who are old and have outlived physical beauty. Ours is a culture of youth and MTV, hipness and things disposable. We're not quite sure how to deal with, or what to think about, things that last. There are so few of them, we often ignore them. I think that's a shame.

My grandmother's still the same person she always was. Just older than most people ever get to be. A deeper well from which to garner knowledge and the wisdom that comes from a long life.

Her body's old, but her eyes are still as blue and gleam as brightly as they did in 1900. Her speech is still clear and comforting, yet it's a different kind of speech. An older style, that's mostly gone now. It's accented heavily from nearly six decades of living in Texas, and interspersed with graceful phrases. Simple sentences are flowery, much like the English found in old books. But it's not in a book. It's spoken by my grandmother.

Instead of saying she's gonna go out and water her plants in a few minutes, she says she's going to do it "directly." Instead of saying she's running a fever, she says she's "taken a fever." But of all the things she says, I like it best when she talks about that nice little old man who comes and mows her yard.

That nice little old man is about seventy-five, and I point out to her that "the nice little old man" was born about the time she got married.

She has a good laugh, the blue eyes even brighter than before.

"I suppose I am getting to be an old lady, aren't I?"

After the laughter we sit quietly, a ticking clock punctuating the silence.

It occurs to me that, while all my grandmother's friends might be gone now, they'd be glad to know their generation is still well-represented.

THE LEAVING AND THE COMING BACK

(The 1,200-Mile-Long Tentacle)

Funny how a scorned lover can turn nasty on you.

I'd read that somewhere or another, but never really given it much thought 'til the early morning of July 12, 1988, when my wife, Brenda, and I pulled off the road outside of El Paso, took a couple of pictures in front of the "Welcome To New Mexico" sign, and then, more or less unceremoniously, left the state of my birth.

That there might be consequences to leaving had never occurred to me during the previous twelve hours as I had driven from Fort Worth to El Paso, my endurance courtesy of periodic sixteen-ounce Dr. Peppers and a Sony Walkman strapped to my ears. Our car radio had a busted tuning knob.

Actually, I was looking forward to finding the end of the state at the time, a feeling shared by most of those who've ever navigated that stretch of Interstate 10 in the dark.

My aunt had warned me that driving this particular road was like pulling on a string hanging from a sweater. "Damnedest thing you ever seen. More you try to get to the end of it, the more there is."

So it was with some degree of relief that we climbed back into the car at the state line and headed west. The rising sun had only served to heighten my awareness of how stupid it'd been to do what I'd just done, and so it was agreed Brenda would drive for a few hours.

I asked only that she wake me at the Arizona line, then climbed into the right seat, and became immediately and blissfully comatose.

I don't know, I guess you could call it the twenty-seven-year-itch. Having lived in Texas for all that time, I just wanted to see what other places had to offer. Being in the advertising business, and owing to a pretty much chronic shortage of copywriters, this was something rather easily accomplished.

I hooked up with a headhunter out of New York, who in turn hooked me up with an agency called Chiat/Day in Venice, California. Phone calls were made, surreptitious weekend interview trips were taken, salary was negotiated, and, voilà, just like Jeb, Granny, Jethro, and Ellie May, I was on my way to California.

My partner at my old agency, using the vernacular of *Bull Durham*, said I was going to "the show." My days in the backwater done, I was headed for the big leagues, and he made no secret that he was just a little envious.

Funny thing was, he'd only recently returned from a similar stint in "the bigs" up in Chicago. He, a native Texan like myself, had spent only one year in Illinois before returning home. It never occurred to me to ask him why he came back so soon, and even if I had, and was then made privy to his tale of woe, I probably would have listened to none of it. I was going come hell or high water. What I didn't know, though, was there was a good measure of both in store for me.

After spending the night in Phoenix, we were up at four the next morning and back on the road for the final leg. Cruising west on I-10 in the darkness, my Walkman tuned to a Mexican radio station, I was full of anticipation, blissfully unaware of the long, ever uncoiling, tentacle—like something out of *Alien* firmly and irrevocably attached to the rear bumper of my 1983 Honda Accord. The other end was planted firmly right under the "X" on the Texas state road map. Said tentacle was perfectly content to stretch just as far as I cared to take it, but had no intention of letting go. Depending on its mood, it would periodically be inclined to twitch or flex its muscle a bit, just to let me know that it, and not I, was in control. To this twitching of the forlorn tentacle, I would attribute the event which coincided with our arrival into the state of California. Events, which I to this day refer to simply as "The Border Incident."

I first saw it as we descended the hill down towards the Colorado River. It seemed harmless enough, just a sign that read, "State of California Agriculture Inspection Station Ahead." I didn't think much of it, having all but forgotten about the three house plants we had in the back seat.

Just after pulling into the toll plaza-like structure, I saw the uniformed attendant gaze lustfully at Brenda's beloved ficus tree, a gift from her grandmother.

He asked about it.

"Is that plant in potting soil or native Texas soil?"

How the hell was I supposed to know? What the hell difference did it make, anyway?

"The State of California currently has a quarantine against out-of-state soil being brought in because it brings in plant diseases that could be a danger to agriculture here," our friendly civil servant explained in a rather detached manner.

"Could you pull over, please?"

"Here we go," I thought to myself. The tentacle squeezed just a little bit harder.

Brenda's eyes were like saucers as this servant of all that is good and noble in the plant world informed us he was confiscating two of our three plants. While he was at it, he also did me the courtesy of telling me those two empty beer bottles on the back floorboard could get me in a good deal of trouble, as well.

"Drive carefully," our friend advised as we pulled away minus two of the three innocent plants that had begun the journey with us. Brenda was in tears. I was left to think about the coarseness of the red carpet that welcomed us to the Golden State. I had the funny feeling this was an omen.

The first town on that side of the river was, ironically enough, Blythe, and we pulled off the interstate for gas and a stop at an Albertson's grocery store for a couple of things Brenda needed, not the least of which was a box of tissues to dry her eyes. She was still grieving over the loss of the plants.

So there we were, standing in the checkout line behind a Mexican lady and her husband at 7:30 in the morning, when the lady faints and falls over, her head hitting the tiled floor with a sound like a bowling ball dropped prematurely on the lane.

The man acted like there was nothing unusual about his wife's collapse. So Brenda ran over and made use of her first aid training, checking her pulse and her breathing. About the time an ambulance arrived, the lady came to and we made our escape, Brenda remarking that the woman didn't smell particularly good and that her husband didn't seem all that worried about her, anyway.

I don't know. Maybe the smell had something to do with his indifference.

Regardless, I heeded the advice of our friendly local protector of native plant life and threw the two beer bottles into a convenient dumpster as we got back to the car. I looked at the label on the side of the dumpster. It belonged to Palo Verde Waste Management. I reflected that they would most likely be the ones who soon would take possession of the felonious ficus and the law-breaking ligustrum. My only hope was that some good soul who lived in Arizona would take pity on the homeless house plants, take them in, and give them a loving home.

Native Texas soil was not welcome in this state. Maybe I should've given more serious thought to this, but as it was, I just got back in the car and continued on.

Was somebody trying to tell me something?

Naaah.

On across the low desert we went, taking little note of the passing landscape until just before we reached Palm Springs. It was there that we saw it. Up in the distance. The brown cloud. You couldn't miss it. Just the other side of the mountains, on an otherwise cloudless blue day, this huge, ugly thing looming right there in front of us.

This was where we were going to make our home?

We continued driving. There was obvious irony, but little comfort in knowing this state, which so jealously guarded against the entrance of unwanted plant life, was perfectly content to allow its people to live life under such a disgusting airborne veil.

Then there was the truck driver.

Coming down the hill from Banning towards the Los Angeles basin, we found ourselves in the middle of the kind of traffic one most commonly associates with southern California: five or six lanes of traffic, one car right behind the other. We were moving along at a fairly reasonable pace, when in my rearview mirror, I saw this eighteen-wheeler weaving in and out of traffic like it was a VW bug. This guy must have been doing eighty if he was doing anything and he was getting uncomfortably close. I moved over into the far left lane—

which was forbidden for trucks—and was hoping for the best, when off to the right I saw him veer over into the outside lane and run up the back end of a Volvo. A couple of the cars behind him crashed into the back of his trailer as he hit the car. I just went on, only halfway kiddingly thinking to myself about taking the next exit and turning this baby around.

Ignoring my better judgment, we drove the rest of the way and finally made it to the apartment the agency had set up for us in Marina Del Rey. I got out and unloaded the trunk.

Was that the slime from a tentacle I saw on the rear bumper as I took the suitcases out?

That night, I sat in the "corporate apartment," wrote in my nearly-semi-daily journal, and listened to the LA country radio station. I hadn't been much on this kind of music, rarely listening to the stations that purported to play this sound, but here in this very foreign land, I found it somehow comforting.

Then it was omen time again.

Jerry Jeff Walker's "LA Freeway" came on. The part where he says, "If I could just get off of this LA freeway without gettin' killed or caught," got me reflecting again on the events of the day just passed. "

Oh well," I thought, "things will get better once we find a permanent place to live and my new job gets underway."

My new employer, Chiat/Day, was, to say the least, an interesting place. The building itself was an old converted warehouse, designed and furnished by well-known and any-thing-but-orthodox architect, Frank Gehry. It was vibrant and exciting, with all its exposed air ducts and wall framing. It was certainly different—and appropriate for a place whose occupants made a living stretching their imaginations to the outer limits.

That was all fine and well and good. My only problem with the place was its location—one of the slummiest, and, sometimes, most dangerous places in Venice.

Granted, it was only two blocks to the beach, for those willing to run the obstacle course of belligerent panhandlers, winos, and public urinaters who made up a substantial portion of the indigenous population in that part of town.

A great number of the people around the place just seemed to take it all in stride and considered the indigents, along with omnipresent graffiti and terminal squalor, a quaint little part of the local color. Never mind that the color in question was the ashen gray of a not-so-recently deceased corpse. It was color, and that was all that mattered.

The prevailing attitude around the office was, "Hey, this is atmosphere. Most people would give their right arm to be working at this agency. We should all be able to overlook the occasional drive-by shooting and robbery/rape."

On the positive side, these first few days at the office helped us to eliminate immediately some areas from our home search— namely, anyplace within a ten-mile radius of the office.

Most of the places we visited in other parts of town offered the intoxicating lure of ratty shag carpet, punctuated with views of neighbors' out-hung laundry blowing lazily in the rust-colored air. For the most part, all that annoying traffic noise would be drowned out effectively by the constant din of screaming infants in the apartment next door, or the odd semi-automatic weapons fire from down the street. And for all this, you paid only in the neighborhood of $1,100 a month.

Fortunately, the parents of a girl at the office owned a fourplex just off Wilshire Boulevard, near Beverly Hills, which had an open unit, complete with washer and dryer connections. And since I worked for the same agency their daughter did, they were willing to forego security deposits and knock a pretty sizable chunk off the monthly rent payment.

We took it.

It was with no small measure of satisfaction that I drove to our new home from the office that first night. Somehow, this seemed like the corner that needed to be turned to make things start working out. The neighborhood seemed stable enough, a judgment I made based solely on the minimal presence of graffiti, which graced the occasional fire hydrant or street light, but did not adorn the sides of moving buses or delivery trucks as it did in other parts of town. Like Venice.

Unfortunately, my visions of Ward coming home to a waiting June, replete with slippers, paper, and pipe, were unceremoniously snuffed out. I arrived home to find Brenda upset about a short afternoon walk she'd taken to the bank up the street, during which she was approached by a kid of about fourteen, who looked directly at her, and, without hesitation, repeatedly grabbed himself in a place on his body not normally grabbed at in public by people who are not professional baseball players.

I tried to calm her as best I could and then set about hooking up the washer and dryer to the connections we were so excited about.

The connections were gas.

The washer and dryer were electric.

On the plus side, the seemingly endless string of foibles in the domestic arena did not extend to the office. Everyone there had been friendly. And despite what surely must have been my alien appearance, everyone welcomed the guy in the Wranglers and cowboy boots with the seemingly endless supply of starched, white button-down shirts and the abnormally normal haircut.

It appeared that, as promised, we would be allowed to do great work without the hindrances to creative thinking often found at large advertising agencies. For this, I was indeed grateful. Especially as September turned into October and the Santa Ana wind brought temperatures that rose as high as 110 degrees, rendering indoor work, even on weekends, a not entirely undesirable alternative.

For two weeks it was like that. Not that 110 degrees is anything I'd never experienced in Texas. I had. What I was not prepared for was the way the easterly blowing Santa Anas took the stagnant brown air, normally blown away from the beach and into town, and deposited it right atop Venice, creating a strange airborne brew that was part car exhaust, part industrial waste, and part coastal fog. It made the air thick, with a consistency much like that of a glass of chocolate milk into which not quite enough Ovaltine has been placed.

There were times when I actually thought this must be somehow similar to the atmosphere one might encounter on Mars, an observation which was in no way countered by the appearances of many of those I passed on the streets driving to and from work each day.

Who knows, maybe they thought me strange, with the end of that big, long, ever-present tentacle trailing along behind my car wherever I went.

I just kept telling myself, like everyone else who worked in this place, how lucky I was to be living here, what a great opportunity this was, and how any number of people at my old company would kill just to be here. And as I turned from Rose Avenue onto Hampton Drive, and saw a man throwing a brick through the window of a Saab with personalized plates, it occurred to me that killing might indeed be one of the prerequisites of survival here.

That is, if the earthquakes didn't get you first.

Now I'd given plenty of thought to them before I came out, but having never experienced one, found it hard to imagine that they could be all that scary. The way I looked at it, if it was all that terrible, why were all these hoardes of people still living here? If, after all, it was so scary, even this flow of lemmings known as California immigrants, of which I was admittedly a part, would have long ago ceased.

That was the argument I made to myself on an almost daily basis, and one in which I took great comfort.

It was not long after that I became the recipient of a 5.2 magnitude rebuttal to said argument.

I guess it was about 3:30 in the morning when I awoke to the sound of the bedroom door dancing back and forth in its frame, as if someone was attempting to kick it in. Shaking the cobwebs out of my head, I realized that kicking the door in would have been an exceedingly stupid thing for anyone to do, since the door was not locked.

The door danced for a few more seconds, that seemed more like minutes, and then stopped. The short silence that followed was interrupted by a chorus of what must have been 300 car alarms up and down Orange Street. This, I think, was my first realization of what someone at work had meant when they called these car alarms the state bird of California.

Actually, I think it was the alarms, and not the earthquake itself, that woke Brenda up. She asked what was going on, and when I told her she'd just slept through her first earthquake, she seemed a little disappointed.

I rose and took a walk around the house to make sure nothing had been knocked over and found no casualties. The only damage was done to our cat's psyche—Wylie had wedged himself firmly into a tiny gap between the commode and the tile wall in the bathroom. Just below him was a still-widening puddle which offered firm evidence of his dislike for California's geophysical situation.

On the one hand, I was glad to have at least experienced an earthquake—especially a relatively harmless one. But that having been said, I was strongly of the opinion that if I were to never experience another, I would be not at all disappointed.

Of course, there were other quakes. The most notable of which came while I was watching the news one evening in January, our sixth month there. Brenda was up in San Francisco at the time and I was sitting on the side of a chair in the den, having just viewed a consumer report about a company that was marketing bogus "earthquake detectors," which looked suspiciously like smoke detectors and were placed at the top of an interior door frame by unsuspecting customers of the swindlers.

As the sports came on and a fellow named "Vic The Brick" delivered his bombastic call of the Laker highlights, I heard the entire house start creaking like one great big garage door in need of WD-40. I glanced down on the floor where the cat was standing and noticed what looked like waves rolling through it.

I looked back at the TV. Even the normally unflappable "Vic The Brick" had stopped talking. He was warily eyeing the klieg lights above him and finally asked, "Is it just me, or are we having an earthquake?"

I assured Vic that it wasn't just him as I made my way to the door, not at all content to see our 1920s vintage fourplex end its days atop my head.

The cat seemed to agree.

About the time we got to the door, the shaking stopped—at least the shaking of the earth stopped. I continued to quiver a good deal longer. Something in the neighborhood of another week to ten days, I think it was.

All in all, that period during 1988 and 1989 while we were living in California was one of the most seismically active periods in that part of the world in quite some time. Nobody from Cal Tech had any plausible explanations for all the quakes, but I had a theory of my own and each new shaker served only to strengthen my belief in it.

It, of course, had nothing to do with fault lines or plate pressure or the like. Mine was the tentacle theory. It was still there, occasionally gripping at me just a little bit tighter, and in doing so, would set the ground to shaking violently. The tentacle still hadn't forgiven me for my attempted getaway and it was now clear it would not be satiated until I made my way back home, repentant.

Yeah, it was still there, and I was starting to lose the battle.

It got even worse when things at the office began to deteriorate. Up until about October we had managed to do some pretty good work. And with the exception of a television commercial that was to have aired nationally on Monday Night Football and was killed at the last minute, most of the really good stuff we had done made it through the labyrinth of agency creative directors and client approvals.

Then they—the ominous, anonymous powers-that-be—went and fired the guy who had hired me and about a dozen or so other people who had started when I did. I didn't know whether there was any correlation between the two, but I remained hopeful about who the replacement would be—right up to the moment I met him.

He was a New Yorker, about fifty or so, with a beard and a pony tail. Pony tails are big in the advertising business. And I'd gotten used to younger guys into this pony tail thing, but I found it hard to get used to a guy his age wearing one. I suppose he felt the pony tail in back somehow compensated for his lack of hair up front.

In addition to the pony tail, he accessorized with these little half-glasses that I never once saw him actually wear. He just kept them dangling there from a little black string around his neck. A place where, the more I got to know the man, I often fantasized about placing a string of my own, with an entirely different and more sinister purpose.

His name was Bob, but most of us called him Dick for short. He was from "the don't rock the boat" school of advertising, one of said institution's fundamental beliefs being, "'tis better the boat be not rocked, lest ye forfeit millions of dollars in billings."

This, of course, was all fine, unless you had the ludicrous and misguided idea—as many of us in the creative department did—that our job was to grab the public's attention. Such radical assertions did not sit well with the car company for which we worked. Thus, the edict came down from on high that were to do as we were told—and enjoy it.

It was Bob, Dick-for-short, who delivered the edict, and seemed not at all unwilling to go along. Almost overnight, the catch phrase of the agency went from "good enough is not enough" to "good enough."

And seeing as the client in question was a large group of car dealers, giving the client what they wanted meant giving them schlock, yell-at-you kinds of commercials that make professional wrestling look like high art.

I guess that was the proverbial straw. Following as it did the earthquakes, the fainting ladies, mad truck drivers, border inspection agents, brown air, and abusive street people, I turned my eyes back to Texas. This California place into which I had so boldly transplanted myself, my wife, and my career only a few months before, was clearly flawed. The tentacle would have its way and I was nothing less than a fool for thinking otherwise.

I guess I made the final decision to return the weekend I took a trip back home to visit friends and family. It was February, and even in their leafless, twisted, wrought-iron looking state, the native post oak trees that covered the hills near my parents' house, seemed far more inviting than any palm or eucalyptus could ever hope to.

I gorged on real Tex-Mex food for the first time in too long and answered myriad questions from would-be followers of my path to California. Without being overly negative, I tried to hose down the assorted fires of enthusiasm with appropriate amounts of reality from one who'd made the trip, gotten past the chamber of commerce clippings, and not been overly impressed. But short of first-hand experience, those fires are not easily extinguished, and I, more than anyone, knew this well.

Climbing on the plane back to Los Angeles, I found myself seated next to a lady from Midland, who, five or six years before, had moved out to Hell On Earth herself. Like me, she'd been seeking bigger and better things, but had not been entirely convinced that Southern California was where those bigger and better things actually were.

We talked most of the way. We laughed about things we missed and those we did not miss about home, the former list being a good deal longer than the latter. We spoke of the traffic, the smog, the earthquakes, and other expatriates we'd met during our stay.

I asked her if she ever thought about coming back. She said she did, but it was something which had long since become an impossibility, at least for the foreseeable future.

She'd finally been able to buy a house. A two-bedroom fixer-upper that backed up to the 405 freeway, which she'd practically stolen for $295,000. It had been broken into four times already, and there was a crack house four doors down, but it helped with her taxes.

Didn't do much for her nerves, though.

I told her about my theory with the tentacle. To my surprise, she didn't judge me a nut, but said she knew of what I spoke, although for her it had always been more of a bungee cord. It had attached itself to her much like the tentacle had to me. She made mention of disasters similar to mine in the early days of her journey, and spoke of sitting on the side of the freeway one morning, reduced to tears at the mere thought of dealing with it all every morning.

Despite the ministrations of the bungee cord, the house she'd bought now had her firmly entrenched, at least for a while—no matter how hard it tried to pull her back.

"I really can't go back now," she said.

"Maybe if I was in your position, I would."

"I'm old and stupid. You're just young and didn't know any better. I guess the good news for you is, you can still do something about it."

I never did ask her name, nor did she ask mine. And after the DC-10 Luxury Liner taxied into gate 49A at LAX, we just got up and headed our respective ways.

"Good luck Mr. Tentacle," she said.

"Same to you, Ms. Bungee Cord."

Not half-an-hour later, as I drove down through the Baldwin Hills on La Cienega, I glanced over at the pump jacks in the seemingly out-of-place oil field that sits there, and noticed what felt like a flat tire. It was then that I noticed everyone else on the road seemed to have a flat tire as well—four to a car as a matter of fact.

No sooner had I set foot back into this sorry place, this sorry place had decided to start moving again. The tremor was short-lived, though, and since no one's tires were actually flattened, traffic began to move—or more accurately—not to move, as usual.

I got home and flipped on the news. Not unexpectedly, they were talking about this recent quake. 5.0. Nothing major. Certainly not the big one. This one hadn't even been centered on the notorious San Andreas fault. In fact, the seismologists over at Cal Tech were just a little baffled by the whole thing because of the unusual location of the epicenter—some mountain over in the San Bernardino range.

Texas Peak, they called it.

This was one omen too many to suit me.

I called Bekins, Mayflower, and United Van Lines the next morning for estimates. Brenda helped dial.

Although she'd never been much for the whole idea of going out there in the first place, she'd good-naturedly gone along with it, no doubt knowing what the outcome would be long before I was willing to admit it.

I went about the various tasks of quitting my job, telling the landlord, telling my mother, and calling my old boss to see if I could get my previous job back.

My mother and the old boss seemed well-pleased with the turn of events. My landlord and employer were not.

A couple of days after my resignation went into effect, my coworkers from Chiat/Day threw me a big going-away lunch. Afterwards, I went home and blasted my stereo, since everyone else was still at work.

I played my favorite Emmylou Harris and Dwight Yoakam (how could he stand to live here?) while leaning back in a chair on the front porch. I noticed for the first time in a very long time what a beautiful day it was.

Funny, but I'd never realized how much prettier this place is when you don't live here. I guess the tentacle was an honorable enough sort not to squeeze a man when he'd already conceded defeat, and so it was that the rest of our days went pretty much without travail.

In less than a week, we'd packed what essentials we'd need into the same car that had brought us there—only now it had California tags.

That night, we stopped over in Blythe, the scene of our grand entry into this paradise. The only reason for the stop was a burning desire on my part to view my exit from this place in the full light of day.

Early the next morning we did just that, my better judgment dissuading me from finding an empty beer bottle and hurling it at the State of California Agricultural Inspection Station as we drove by.

Crossing the Colorado River into Arizona, I breathed a sigh of relief and vowed to not stop driving until we passed the first "Don't Mess With Texas" sign.

I didn't want the tentacle to get the wrong idea, and was determined to make certain it understood I was headed back home and would stray no more. Besides, I didn't like all that slime on the bumper.

Twelve hours later, we'd gassed up the car in Las Cruces and continued east in the twilight.

Shortly after crossing the state line back into Texas, some fellow in a pickup truck, having seen our California tags, sped by and flipped us the finger.

As he went around, I noticed the NRA sticker on his back window, and another on his bumper that read, "Feed Jane Fonda To The Whales."

Man it felt good to be home.

PEOPLE WHO STICK

TO THE ROOF

OF YOUR MIND

———————————

This old porch is just a weathered, gray-haired seventy years of
  Texas.
He's doin' all he can not to give into the city.
And he always takes the rent late, so long as I run his cattle.
He picks me up at dinner time, I listen to him rattle.
He says, "The Brazos still runs muddy like she's runned all along.
There ain't never been no cane to grind, the cotton's all but gone.
And you know, that Chevrolet pickup, she was somethin' back in
  '60.
Now there won't nobody listen to him, 'cause they all think he's
  crazy.

———————

Robert Earl Keen, Jr., and Lyle Lovett
"The Front Porch Song"

TYNCE LOOMIS

Tynce Loomis would get drunk on Schlitz Beer and
drive up and down the road in his primer-colored 1970
Nova SS looking for people to follow.

Nobody in his little part of Palo Pinto County knew why
he did it, or what kind of alcohol-shaded logic was behind his
habit, they just knew that he did it. And since it never went
beyond that, most of the locals wrote it off as a just another
one of the peculiarities of a man who ran out of sanity before
he got to the grave.

According to Tynce's estranged daughter, Dottie, carbon
dating techniques placed Tynce Loomis's age at somewhere
in the neighborhood of eighty. Although she was quick to add
he didn't look a day over ninety-five.

His white flattop haircut sat atop a face with more lines than
a Wal-Mart on Saturday morning. And those few teeth that
had not already given up the ghost showed the residual effects
of a lifelong love affair with W.E. Garrett finely ground snuff,
a tryst he still carried on with some prejudice.

The old man's family didn't come around much anymore.
In fact, Dottie, a registered nurse in Mineral Wells and his

only daughter, just made the journey out to his trailer peri-odically to "make sure he hadn't got hissef or someone else kilt yet."

Dottie always said "yet" in a way that suggested "some-one's" getting killed was an inevitability which had long since been accepted by all concerned. Actually, Dottie herself came close to doing him in about fifteen or so years ago on one of her sporadic trips out to see him.

He'd gotten even more drunked up than usual and had refused to allow her entry to his beloved double-wide. Finally, she rather undaintily gained access through a bedroom win-dow, ascending a rusted-out Frigidaire icebox that had lan-guished next to the trailer since the early years of the Truman administration.

When she got into the house, she surprised the old man, who was still watching the front door from the comfort of his Barcalounger. His perpetually blurry aim rendered the single-shot .410 he held lovingly across his chest ineffectual.

Tynce saw Dottie as she came around the corner, but when he tried to upright the recliner, he instead hit the electric back massager button. The stream of cuss word-laced vitriol he spewed at her took on a Linda Blair-esque feel as the vibrating of the back massager distorted his already raspy voice. Tynce continued his diatribe as he tried to shut the back massager off and upright himself. Dottie seized the opportunity to wrest the .410 out of his lap. As the Palo Pinto County sheriff's investigating officer would later state in his incident report, "this was not an advisable move."

She did, in fact, get hold of the butt of the .410 and moved the trigger out of harm's (read Tynce's) reach. He would have none of this, however, and gripped the business end of the weapon, refusing to let go.

For the next few minutes, this bizarre tug of war went on, accompanied by the sounds of Tynce's ceaseless cussing, the barking of his part-dachshund, part-poodle dog, Rat, and the audio from a *Gomer Pyle USMC* rerun.

The presence of the Palo Pinto County sheriff's officer was necessitated when Tynce finally let go, sending Dottie back into a stack of fifteen years worth of the Sunday *Fort Worth Star-Telegram*. That's when her finger hit the trigger, firing a glancing volley off the old man's left shoulder.

Mrs. Tankersly down the road heard the shot and knew immediately from whence it had come. She called the sheriff, halfway hoping Tynce had finally done himself in. Later she related to Mrs. Bates up at church services that God watches out for drunks and fools, so Tynce Loomis was doubly protected and likely to outlive everyone.

Of course, he refused to be taken into town, only grudgingly allowing one of the paramedics to bandage him up while totally refusing entrance to the other because she was a woman, and "weren't no woman doctor gonna touch him as long as he was anywheres over room temperature."

The incident grew to legendary proportions around town. And as such stories are wont to do, each new telling added a new layer of embellishment, the thickness of which almost always varied depending upon the imagination of the story-teller.

Presumably in the interest of high drama, all the accidental aspects of the episode had been removed when I first heard the story in 1987. By then it had evolved into something like, "Old crazy Tynce Loomis had tried to kill his daughter 'cause she interrupted the *Gomer Pyle Show* on TV one afternoon and she'd had to shoot the old man in self-defense." The running joke associated with this story was that the district attorney had considered charging her with aggravated criminal negligence—for not aiming better.

I had to assume this was yet another layer of embellishment, as embellishment is second only to oil as a natural resource in this part of the world.

It turned out that Tynce Loomis healed up just fine, and in a matter of less than a week, was back out following people again in his Nova. Sometimes he traveled the road between Graford and Palo Pinto, the blacktop to which his driveway was connected, and sometimes, when he got adventurous, he'd get on down to old 180 that ran between Mineral Wells and Breckenridge.

To say that he was an interesting sight behind the wheel of a car is an understatement. The Nova, which had formerly belonged to one of his grandsons, was the type driven with great passion by teenagers during the 1970s. It sported rear mag wheels and had been wrecked so many times, it was referred to as "The BondoMobile" by the younger members of the family.

If there was a muffler on the thing, it certainly was not obvious. The inspection sticker, long since expired, didn't resemble any that had been issued by the State of Texas in the last ten years, although an imaginative someone had made an abortive attempt at counterfeiting a new month and year onto the sticker with a felt pen.

The car's worn-out suspension mimicked a squeaky bed frame being used for amorous purposes. Even several seconds after the ignition had been shut off and the engine had coughed itself silent, you'd still hear it. Especially when the old man would get out. Slamming the door perpetuated the noise for what seemed like several minutes.

It was that squeaking sound that first signaled Tynce Loomis's uninvited arrival into my life.

I'd long wanted a piece of land—fifty or a hundred acres, within a couple of hours of home. An easy drive on a Friday evening. I'd further decided that, if there was s small house of some sort on the premises, so much the better. Didn't need to be anything special, just functional enough for occasional head-clearing and thought inducement.

The place I found was in the shadow of the Palo Pinto Mountains (hills if you're from Colorado or New Mexico) west of Mineral Wells. The little red flagstone house with well and septic tank sat in the middle of a hundred acres, heavily peppered with mesquite and prickly pear. It was bordered on the north and west by a fairly substantial cattle ranching concern. To the south was another, mostly absentee owner like myself, and to the east, back toward the road, my newfound think tank slash moneypit was bordered by a fairly thin parcel of land occupied only by a trailer and a few itinerant pieces of rotting appliances and ranch implements.

It was Tynce Loomis's place, a fact that was made clear to me one fine fall evening as I lay on the hood of my truck near the fence line between my property and his. I'd come out to do nothing more than watch the sun set over the top of Shut-In Mountain, and enjoy a cold beer.

That's when I heard the squeaking. And I guess it went on for at least ten minutes before the Nova came bouncing into sight out of the bottom of a dry ravine.

I remember thinking, "I guess that's one thing about having a car like that, pretty much no matter what you do to it, chances are worse has been done to it before, so it just doesn't matter."

Plainly it didn't matter to him. He kept hitting the gas and letting up on it in a very irritating fashion as he rolled over anything that got between him and where it was he was going. Rocks, flora, fauna, the local pastor, it didn't matter what you were if you were in his way; your prayers had best been said.

Finally, he pulled up to the fence and just sat there. So much for enjoying a nice quiet sunset alone. And to make it all that much more bothersome, the old man didn't say anything. He just kept clearing his throat in the disgusting way that old men do. The more time went on, the more he did it.

I'd glance back at him once in a while through the windshield of my truck and nod my head. With the orange glow of the sun on his face and his eyes squinted, he looked like one of those Chinese Sharpei dogs with a piece of white Velcro on top of his head.

I was, as yet, a virgin to the gossip, including the stories about Tynce Loomis, so I decided to be neighborly, walk over, and talk to him across the fence.

I jumped off the hood and headed over in the twilight. I had gotten about as far as the back bumper when the old Nova started, did a quick 180, and roared back down into the ravine, the irritating, rhythmic punching of the gas peddle continuing as it had before.

"Pleased to meet you," I said to the dust.

In the ensuing weekends, it almost became a ritual. Me driving out to the edge of my property and sitting on the hood of my truck as the sun went down, and the old man driving his old Nova out to the edge of his property and watching me watch the sunset. He never said anything and always left abruptly if I even made a move his way—a habit which I broke myself of after the third unsuccessful, and obviously futile, attempt.

I didn't get out to the place over the winter much, at least not for whole weekends at a time, and thus largely forgot about the bizarre little episodes. Then, one Saturday night in March,

I returned to my old perch to watch a hellacious line of thunderstorms way out to the west. As I sat and watched the light show in the thick spring air, I heard the squeaking again. As before, it stopped just the other side of my fence. I didn't bother to look at the source. I knew it was Tynce. I could feel his stare burning the back of my head.

This time there was a twist, though. After about twenty minutes of sitting there, he laid on his horn. Startled—who knew that anything as luxurious as a horn actually worked on the old man's car?— I turned and faced him briefly. Figuring it had just been an accident, I went back to watching God's own laser show.

Tynce Loomis laid on his horn again, and this time he stayed on it.

Having had enough, and surmising that the alien being wanted to communicate, I walked on over. This time, he didn't leave, just looked at me, his face and flattop taking on a surreal—no, check that—scary quality as the lightning flashes in the distance reflected off it.

I leaned into one of the posts along the barbed wire fence that separated us.

"Howdy," I said in a nervous sort of way I could only compare to that leery feeling you get around an unknown and potentially fierce dog.

As if my greeting were neither heard nor necessary, he just began talking.

"That weatherman Harold Taft on the TeeV says we 'sposed to get one hellacious bump after while. Baseball-sized hail over t'other side of Bray-kin-ridge. What do you think of Harold Taft? You like him better 'an that summich with the bow tie?"

Even as I prepared a thoughtful answer, he continued on, a toothless, eighty-year-old run-on sentence with no periods in sight.

"You don't live out here all the time, do you?"

"No, I just..."

"Just like to come here, drink yer beer, and pee off the porch, I know how ye are, get tired of living in one of them cul-dee-sacs with all them snotty-nosed kids and neighbors borrowin' the lawn mower, so you come out here and pretend youse some kind of ag-man or horse fella or some such, most of 'em horse's asses if you ask me, which I'm well aware you didn't, but I always like to let people know where I stand, since that ways, they'll know where not to spit, if you folla what I's sayin'."

Attempting to drive a wedge between the old man's free-flowing sentences, I said, "Well—

"He said he hoped I didn't mind him watching me over the past few months without being overly friendly, adding that he "didn't mean no offense, but just wanted to make sure I wasn't some kind of 'har-mo-sexual, or devil worshipper or the like."

Finally managing to get a couple of responses in, I assured him I was neither, to which he replied, "Somebody over at

Millsap found pentygrams carved into the sides of a couple of his heifers not long ago, so you never know."

Finding this to be a point we could, indeed, agree upon, I nodded my head, having thrown in the towel in regard to attempting a complete sentence.

Tynce Loomis spat through the window of his 1970 Nova SS Coupe, started it up, and drove off, having long since deemed unnecessary the hellos and good-byes normally used to begin and end civil conversations.

I learned back up against the fence post and watched the lightning dance off his nonpaint job as he drove away. He didn't use his headlights and his darkened rear license plate, which was suspended only by one screw in the top left corner, periodically bounced off the ground—depending on the size of the bump, tree, or unfortunate Homo sapiens he hit.

That was the first of many such fence-post meetings I was to have with Tynce Loomis over the next few months. At the time, I hadn't heard all the stories about the old man and so was not nearly as reluctant as most would've been to have any dealings with him.

The more I listened to him talk—which is about all I had the opportunity to do—the more I got to kind of like him. Oh, he was terribly prejudiced and highly intoxicated most of the time, but it was like talking to someone who had died during the last century and come back to open a window long shut, affording me a private showing of how things used to be.

He knew countless stories about the people who had been the previous owners of the land on which we stood. He loved to talk about the old settlers and the battles they fought with the Comanches. Once you got him onto one of those, he'd just keep going.

After hearing some of the stories about him and his hermit-like leanings, I asked him one night why he was so violently opposed to socializing, but felt at ease coming out and talking to me.

He spat. He was always doing that. Then he belched. He was always doing that, too.

"Well," he said, "the one thing I noticed about you when you went to comin' out here was that you usually come by yusef."

"Yeah, well, sometimes I bring my wife with me," I said.

"Hell, I didn't say you didn't," he rebutted, "but most of the damn time, it's just you. I like that. You come out here alone, but you don't get lonesome, do you?"

"No."

"That's what I mean, you come out here to just sit and think, with nobody to talk to but yuself. I like that in a man. Shows you ain't afraid of being stuck with nobody to entertain you other than you. There's a helluva lot to be said for that. Most people just don't understand that, though.

"Hell, I raised a family. I had a good wife, God rest her sweet soul. I done all that in-law stuff. I wooped my kids when they done bad and told 'em when they done good. I lived a good full life. But the one thing I didn't do was to get to know Tynce Loomis. So now that I'm old and probly ain't got that much more time, I'm just enjoying my own company a little bit.

"If you asked me, solitude ain't never been given its due as a way of carryin' on a life. I like it. So when I seen that you was a fella who didn't seem to be scared of it, I kinda figured you'd been someone I could take to. Generally a fella who spends a little time by hissef don't need to hear the sound of his voice jabberin' all the time, which means he's a good listener, and I figured I got some stuff somebody oughta listen to.

"I may be an old drunk without much to account for hisself, but I got a few things in this old head that somebody oughta pay 'tention to. I knowed people in my time who was the first ones to come out here and I think that's worth somethin'.

"Most people don't give much of a damn, and if they don't I've got no need for 'em, but when I run upon somebody who do, I figure I may as well go ahead and let 'em hear what I got to say. You struck me as somebody to who it matters.

"They ain't many like you, and there ain't many like me, that's all."

After that the old man left in his usual manner, I sat on the hood of my truck a good deal longer than usual, thinking about what he'd said.

Solitude, and the thought that comes with it, is looked down upon by the world most of us find ourselves in. I'd certainly been called to task in the past for pursuing it. It's not so much that I was antisocial or didn't like people, it was just that I've always been partial to silence and the thought it provokes.

Most lives are led within the constant blare of the TV and the expectations of others, thus rendering the virtues of aloneness to the outcasts. In the old man, I saw someone who rejected all that. And perhaps someone not unlike who I might eventually become, a thought that both pleased and irritated me.

Regardless, over the next few months, the two loners met religiously at the fence, the older one transmitting the truths and knowledge of eighty-odd years and the younger one listening and not knowing what would be done with the information obtained.

One thick night in May, the old man didn't show. Another line of thunderstorms was moving in from Bray-kin-ridge, and as always I was out there to watch. The next morning, I decided to drive over to the double-wide to check on him.

I'd never been over there before and was struck by the squalor. The door was unlocked, guarded only by Rat the dog, who barked incessantly at my intrusion.

Tynce Loomis was on his Barcalounger, the single-shot .410 in its usual position upon his lap. A Campbell's soup can about half full of the inevitable results of Mr. W.E. Garrett's snuff sat on the shag carpet nearby. The TV rolled. Oprah was exploring some issue of great significance to America. Whatever it was, it struck me as not nearly as important as the fact that Tynce Loomis had finished his time on this earth.

I called his daughter Dottie at the hospital in Mineral Wells and she made all the necessary arrangements.

They buried him out near the Brazos, where he'd told me he used to go "nekkid swimming" with his wife to be. When the preacher was done, I said a few words to the dozen or so who'd showed and assured the gathered he'd accepted Christ and had told me as much before his passing. I told them how he was one of the last of a breed of people who, for better or worse, we don't see much anymore. I spoke, to mostly uninterested looking gazes, about our evening fence talks and of the things that he had passed on to me.

We sang "Amazing Grace" a cappella and it was over. I walked to my truck, gazed off toward Shut-In Mountain, and cried.

In the ensuing days, family members came out to the double-wide and collected what they wanted, remnants of the old man's life. In his handwritten will and testament, he'd given his parcel of mesquite-covered land to Dottie, who agreed to sell it to me and thanked me for comforting him during his last days.

Before the sale cleared escrow, they had the trailer and the accompanying junk cleared off the property. Rat, unwanted by any of the descendants and unwilling to be caught by anyone intending to take him to the pound, took up residence at my place.

Though Tynce's land was now mine, I left up the old barbed wire fence that divided our property in deference to our one-sided late night chats there. And as always, I'd pull up in the evening with a Playmate cooler full of cold beer and inhale the sound of the cicadas and the fragrant scent of cow patties in the spring night air. I figured the old man was watching me, and just hoped there was some part of heaven where a fellow could get off to "hisself" in a place that resembled the Palo Pinto Mountains, and that he didn't mind that I now enjoyed the nighttime view from the hood of a primer-colored 1970 Nova SS with an out-of-date inspection sticker and a rear license plate that dragged the ground.

T he dog raised his head up off the floor when the phone rang. He always did that, as if to alert the old man that it was, in fact, ringing and that something needed to be done about it. With his hearing the way it was, this was pretty much the only way Lamar McKenzie knew anymore when someone was calling. It had been this way for ten or twelve years now, and barring any miracles of modern science, it was unlikely to change.

He got up out of the leather chair, set down his well-used coffee cup, and creaked over to the table where Ma Bell's own nuisance sat demanding immediate attention. As he walked, he made note of the clock on the wall. It was only 5:15 in the morning, for crying out loud.

Along the way, he made sure to turn the radio down, tuned as it always was this time of morning to the ranch and stockman's report on WBAP. It had been years since the main subject of the daily program had been his life's work, but he continued to rise early and turn it on nonetheless. It was habit, plain and simple, and the volume of the radio blasted at a level one would expect of someone who's hearing had all but failed.

On about the eighth ring, he caught the receiver in his liver-spotted hand and stuck it against his face.

"Yello."

The voice on the other end spoke loudly, well aware of the old man's aural handicap.

"Uncle Mar," the voice said, alerting him to the fact that it was the oldest son of his last best friend on the other end of the line.

"We lost Pops last night, and I wanted you to be one of the first to know."

The old man just stood there for a minute, letting the words sink in. He looked over at the dog, who once again raised his head, sensing something was amiss merely by his owner's expression.

"Uncle Mar?" came the disembodied voice.

"Was he at peace when he went?" Lamar McKenzie managed to ask, recalling something he'd once heard a preacher ask in a similar situation.

"Yessir, he was," came the reply.

"Well, y'all let me know about the arrangements and everything."

"Yessir, we sure will."

"Gonna miss him," Lamar offered.

"Yessir, we all will," the voice responded.

The old man hung up the phone and went back to his coffee cup and chair. He offered a brief hand of comfort to the dog as he sat back down and reflected on the phone call.

The decedent was Walt Reedus, the second member of a threesome of lifelong friends, that also had included Billy Fisher and Lamar. Lamar was now the only surviving member of the group.

The legacy weighed heavily on him.

He'd never thought he'd be the last one of them to go. Now ninety-four, he reflected back on the eighty- some-odd years they'd been best buddies. He'd been physically weaker than the other two, less athletic in high school and less handy with cars and things mechanical; he'd also been the most pensive and prone to showing emotion—as much as a fella from his generation could be called emotional. By today's standards that wasn't a heck of a lot. But despite their differences, one would be hard-pressed to find a stronger bond of friendship anywhere.

He recalled the first time he met Walt. It seemed like it must have been about the fifth grade. Lamar had been invited over to another boy's house to play football one afternoon after school. Walt was there, too, a strapping youngster, and the biggest of the three of them.

Lamar arrived to find Walt sitting atop the other two boys, who were screaming for mercy to no avail. Walt just sat there and waved at Lamar as he came over, the sinister smile on his face almost daring Lamar to do something about the situation.

He didn't. Walt was far too big and Lamar was far too smart for that. And from that moment on, he was content to ally himself with the bigger boy and overlook his bullyish tendencies, believing it was better to be on his side than the object of his wrath.

The two boys became a pretty much inseparable duo that would be altered only by the admission of the third member of the group six or seven years later.

Billy Fisher completed the group the summer before they had all gone off to college. High school football had brought Walt and him together and they found they shared a similar sarcastic outlook on life. Billy and Lamar found they also shared common ground: both had determined to attend The University of Texas at Austin in the fall.

Walt, on the other hand, had come from a family of Aggies, and tradition, as much as anything, dictated he would follow the ancestral footprints to Texas A&M in College Station.

For most Texans, this would have meant a parting of the ways. Anyone who's spent any time here knows that the ill will between partisans of the two universities runs deep and bitter, the kind of deep-seated feud that has stood in the way of marriages and caused churches to split up. So it was no small point of amazement to those who witnessed it that no rift occurred. The Aggie and the Longhorns remained no less devoted to one another.

Not only did the three remain friends, they committed a further breach of tradition by trekking back and forth between the two schools for weekend revelries, forging stronger ties and rendering many brain cells useless.

After college, the three had returned to Fort Worth, each eventually marrying and settling down within a few blocks of where they had grown up.

Marriage might well have ended, or at least diminished, their friendship. But, while the sheer amount of time they spent together did become less than before, it was certainly not enough to do them in. Even less than cordial feelings between one wife and the wives of the other two meant not a damn to any of the men.

Even vastly different careers failed to separate them in ways that it might have other, less rooted friendships. As they had throughout college, they continued together for periodic weekend trips to a local pool hall, the evenings usually ending in a summit meeting on the tailgate of whoever's pickup truck they happened to be in that night, in front of whoever's house it was they stopped at first.

More than once the police had been called to investigate a noise complaint. More often then not, the patrol officer was someone they'd gone to school with who ended up officially giving them a warning, and unofficially sticking around a few minutes to catch up on old times.

There was also the annual fishing trip, that was in some years more than annual and in others closer to monthly. During these forays into the wilds, their diets consisted of mostly Ranch Style Beans, Oreos, and hot dogs, washed down with massive quantities of beer. At very few times during these trips were the underwater residents of whichever lake they visited in any kind of danger.

Of course, the fishing wasn't the point. It was simply an excuse to spend time together the way they had when they were younger.

Throughout it all, their discussions with one another were rarely serious. Aside from their occasional forays into politics—on which two of the three almost always agreed, much to the chagrin of the third—little of substance was ever discussed. Even through the deaths of loved ones and times of financial hardship, moral support was provided not by words so much as by simply being together. No words were necessary, no hugs were exchanged. Their friendship was understood. It needed no outward displays. It just was.

This was a point lost on a good many outsiders who viewed the circle of three. It seemed that no matter how bad the situation, the biting, sarcastic exchanges between them never changed, leaving some to wonder what good friends they could be given the way they talked to each other.

But to Lamar, this was precisely the point. All else in life was highly changeable, including the words exchanged between human beings. Even the sacred words of the wedding vow had, in recent years, grown tarnished and unheeded, leaving perhaps the strongest bonds those that are not spoken, but well-understood. It was upon such belief their lifelong friendship had been built, and perhaps why it had survived, unchanged, through eight decades.

This was the epitaph Lamar McKenzie put on their friendship as he sat there in the early morning, finishing the cup of coffee he'd started before the phone call with the news of Walt's passing had interrupted him.

He was left to reflect on what it all meant, and that seemed somehow appropriate since he had always been the one given to considering such things. He thought about the last time he had seen Walt, about a week earlier when they'd checked him into the hospital for a respiratory infection.

Lamar's daughter had driven him to the hospital, where he'd found his old friend with an oxygen mask over his face, a Bob Wills song playing on the tape machine he'd had brought up for him. Lamar thought Walt was asleep, so he sat down in one of the chairs across the room. He was about to nod off himself when Walt had pulled the mask off and jarred him awake.

"Damned good thing we made the Lake Whitney trip last month instead of this one, huh?" he said, the sentence cut off with a brutal coughing fit.

Lamar had just nodded his head and smiled, content to sit and listen to the tape with his friend until visiting hours ended and his daughter drove him back home.

Silence that might have been uncomfortable and awkward between others was not to these two. And now that Lamar alone was left, the silence would not be nearly so hard to endure.

He made a vow to himself to maintain the ritual of the annual fishing excursions in spite of his age. And while he certainly had other friends and relatives who could drive him out there, he determined the bulk of the trips would be spent alone, figuring the memories in his head would provide more companionship than anyone else ever could.

Lamar McKenzie got up and walked outside to observe the beginning of the first day since the fall of 1908 that he had been truly alone.

The dog stood up, revealing a worn spot in the carpet, from many years of napping there, and followed the old man onto the front porch. He sat down next to the old man and looked out in the same general direction as his master, not knowing what he was looking for, but looking nonetheless.

The breaths of both crystallized in the cold morning air. Lamar McKenzie noted that the cloud-streaked sunrise was quiet, and all the more beautiful for it.

A FIBERGLASS SUMMER

A ltee Purvis was screaming at me. Screaming in a kind of high pitched, raspy voice that made it sound as if somebody was running a blade right up his midsection and had no intention of stopping anytime soon.

"Mike, Mike, get over here, man. Get over here."

I'd only met Altee Purvis for the first time about two hours earlier and now it sounded as if I was being called upon to save his life.

I had been bear-hugging huge bales of fiberglass insulation off a Southern Pacific railroad boxcar and throwing them onto a handcart in the hot evening air at the Taggert Insulation warehouse on the eastern outskirts of Austin when I first heard him. Being raised up a good Christian boy, I gladly threw down a bale that seemed to weigh quite a bit more than I did and began making my way through the warehouse toward the screaming.

It was on row four, where they kept the R-30 rockwool bats, that I saw him. He seemed to be doing some sort of demon-possessed dance, his arms flailing wildly and his eyes like saucers against his black skin.

He'd thrown off his Blue Mule work gloves and seemed to be stomping on them as I approached him, making me even less certain if I should call the police, an ambulance, or a priest.

"What's the deal, man?" I asked, continuing toward him.

"Snakes, snakes, five hundred of 'em, a whole nest of 'em," he shrieked, all the while still doing his dance, which now and forever I would know as his snake dance.

His right arm was up around his head, his hand seeming to periodically slap his own face. His left arm, which still flailed wildly, pointed more or less toward one particular stack of insulation bales, so I made my way in that direction.

Fortunately, I had possessed the presence of mind to bring along a big iron bar used to open the railroad cars. With this I pushed back the top couple of bales on the offending pile to see what was really there.

Sure enough, underneath was a squirming, intertwined pile of serpents of undetermined breed. Certainly not five hundred, but quite a few nonetheless. Several weeks of flooding had no doubt run them up into the Taggert Insulation warehouse just off Webberville Road, and the disgusting things had now found homes in the every bit as disgusting rockwool insulation that we found ourselves hefting around every evening.

Fortunately, the big iron bar made quick work of the situation, as I got most of them wrapped around the utensil and chunked them out the back door.

This was not good enough for Altee Purvis, however. He wanted every one of them sent straight to that big rockwool insulation warehouse up in the sky. I understood his feelings, but my better side prevailed, and I just threw them out the other side of the railroad siding around back.

Thus began, and pretty much ended, the first day of work for me and Altee Purvis.

The unlikely pair that was us had been thrown together for the first time earlier that afternoon, as he and I had both applied for, and been accepted as, "warehousemen."

Admittedly, it was a rather grandiose term for a twenty-one-year-old white college kid looking for some extra summer money, and a nineteen-year-old black kid from the bad side of Austin who looked at the whole deal as pretty much a career opportunity.

The job, or career opportunity if you will, entailed us showing up at around the hottest part of the afternoon and spending the next four-and-a-half hours sweating, unloading boxcars, then sweating some more, and loading trucks for the next day's jobs, after which we would sweat a bit more.

Mostly, our work was unsupervised, as everyone else had gone home by the time we got there. So, not coincidentally, we didn't do much more work the day the plague of snakes was visited upon us. In fact, by the time I'd thrown the last of the serpents out, Altee was headed out to his '72 Chevelle SS for a trip down to the Zip-in food store for a couple of forty-ounce Old English 800s.

During his absence, I sat on the edge of the loading dock next to truck number sixty-seven and looked off to the east at the big thunderheads building in the distance. For the first time, I wondered what the hell I was doing here. I mean, if I'd had any sense, I would've gone home for the summer like everyone else and would now be ensconced comfortably in our backyard pool, enjoying the easy life.

Of course, that would have meant forsaking my dream job as a part-time weekend disc jockey at an FM radio station, and the late night phone calls from girls that were the fringe benefits of such a job. I had decided to stay in town and find some way of supplementing my $3.65 an hour income.

Dad had said it was fine with him if I had the ability to pay my own way, but mother had said she felt I was being foolish for getting all caught up in such a thing and should come home like every other decent mother-loving child would do.

Grudgingly, I had begun to think she was right. I sat there, sweating profusely from doing nothing more than trying to pick the little prickly fiberglass things out of my arms, and waited for some crazy black kid to come back with two brown paper bags full of some sort of kick-butt malt liquor.

Drinking on the job on my first day. Yeah, this was gonna be interesting.

The sound of loud dual exhausts and the slamming of Altee's door startled me out of my sudden fit of introspection, and I looked up to see him coming across the dusty parking lot, two malt liquors in one hand and a boom box in the other.

He pulled himself up on the loading dock next to me, handed me one of the brown paper bags and turned on Rick James who sang something about "She's a very freeeaky girl . . ."

"What you doin' down here anyway, college boy?" he started in.

"Saving your black butt from snakes, I guess," I said, just a little bit annoyed by the "college boy" part.

"Bet your mamma and daddy give you all the money you need," he continued, undeterred.

"They help me when I'm going to school, but they don't just throw money at me to stay down here, so I probably need this job just as bad as you do," I said, trying to keep from vomiting at my first sip from the brown bag.

"Them snakes didn't bother you none, did they?" he asked.

"They won't bother you if you don't give 'em any reason to," I said.

"That's cool," he replied, although I didn't know if he was referring to the snakes and their behavior or my attitude toward them.

For the next twenty minutes or so we just sat there, me and Altee Purvis and Rick James on the boom box, until we finished up the Old English 800s and I finally persuaded him that we should probably finish doing what we were supposed to do if we wanted to continue our semi-gainful employment there at the Taggert Insulation warehouse off of Webberville Road.

Fortunately, the next few days brought no more snakes. On the other hand, Altee continued to bring the same boom box and proceeded to play the same Rick James tape ad nauseam. After a time, I'd wait until he went off to the Porta-Can in the parking lot and flip the thing over to the country station. This started a never-ending battle of cultures in which he would wait until I went off to the same Porta-Can and would then turn it back to the tape or over to the soul station.

And in spite of the absence of our serpent friends, we'd still pause in memory of that first day's events and head off to the Zip-in store for liquid refreshment. We took turns going. On my days, we'd have a couple of Coors tall boys and on his days we'd drink malt liquor.

He couldn't understand how I could drink that watery stuff and I couldn't understand how he could drink that coma-inducing stuff, but we always drank what the other had brought, chalking it up to some sort of crude, cross-cultural sensitivity training.

He even got to where Merle Haggard or George Jones didn't make him puke and I more or less got that way about Rick James and the Dazz Band.

Of course, the good people who operated Taggert Insulation didn't have us there for social experimentation and better understanding between the races; they had us there to load trucks and unload boxcars, and in spite of our nightly trips down to the store, we actually developed into a pretty good team.

They kept tabs on us by how many trucks we had fully loaded for the next morning's work, and all in all, we did pretty well. Although the lack of supervision made me feel a little like a character from a Charlie Brown cartoon.

We'd show up, do our work, make our beer run, do more work, lock up, and then go our respective ways—me, going back home for a shower and then off to my job as a nighttime DJ at a local beer joint, and him off to whatever it was he did. One night, after much convincing, I talked him into going with me to my other, more glamorous gig. He'd shown a lot of trepidation at the thought.

"You think there'll be any trouble with a brother coming in over there?" he kept asking.

"It's just like the snakes," I said. "You don't mess with them, they won't mess with you."

"We get in a fight, you gonna cover my backside or you gonna side with them redneck white boys?" he asked.

"I took care of them snakes for you didn't I?"

"That's cool," Altee Purvis said.

Actually, aside from his almost disturbing phobia in regard to snakes, I'd never really thought of Altee as somebody who needed much backside covering. He wasn't particularly tall or anything, but he seemed plenty strong and certainly capable of taking care of himself—and pretty much anyone else who might try to do him ill.

That, along with the economy-sized dose of naïveté I carried around with me at the time, convinced me there would be no trouble in bringing a black guy along with me to the bar where I worked. Never mind that this bar was called the "Why Not" Bar and Lounge. Or that those holes in the walls around the pool tables weren't from errant pool cues, but from purposefully aimed Colts and Remingtons. Or that the "mood lighting" over the dance floor consisted of a string of once multi-colored Noma blinking Christmas lights. Or that management had posted signs in the restrooms requesting patrons to "please refrain from eating the urinal cakes." Or even that people said the name "Why Not" was short for "why not just beat yourself over the head with a tire tool instead, because that's what will happen if you come in here, anyway."

My experience as "the DJ from the country radio station" who played the records and sipped free beer had been much less eventful than the legends I kept hearing about. Consequently, I didn't even think about what I might be inviting by bringing along my black friend to hang out for the evening.

I waited in the gravel parking lot, still itching from the insulation stuck in my arms, and listened to the radio while two drunk guys tried to write their names in the dust as they peed next to their pickup down the way.

Maybe this wasn't such a grand idea after all.

But the time for that sort of thinking ended as the blue Chevelle with dual glass-pack exhausts pulled in singing its inimitable song. The deep bass thumping of his stereo blared out into the evening through the closed windows. Only this time it wasn't Rick James or the Bar-Kays, but something I could've sworn sounded like George Strait.

I got out of my car and walked on over as Altee emerged from his. I caught sight of him and stopped dead in my tracks.

Altee Purvis had turned into Charley Pride, or at least a fair imitation of him.

His brand new eel-skin boots poked out from under his Jordache (or Jo-dash as he called them) jeans, which were cinched up by a western belt with a buckle the size of several northeastern states, and a western shirt. As if to complete the effect, he popped on a four-x, cream-colored felt Stetson hat, and then just stood there and posed.

It was like that scene from *Blazing Saddles* where Cleavon Little rides up in his best Gucci cowboy apparel with the complete Count Basie orchestra playing in the background.

Unfortunately, I wasn't the only one taking in this spectacle. The two guys over by the pickup truck, who had only recently completed their exercise in urinary calligraphy, were now sizing up the whole situation along with me. They didn't seem nearly as amused by the sight, but thankfully kept their distance.

"What you think, Fro?" Altee asked. He'd only recently started shortening my last name and calling me "Fro" for some unknown reason.

"Your Jo-dash are too short with those boots," I snorted, and pushed him along toward the door.

I flicked my eyes up at the flashing neon sign and suddenly could think of quite a number of reasons "why not."

As I opened the door, we were immediately hit by a red, crushed velvet kind of darkness and the sound of a Gary Stewart song blaring at a decibel level that would make most jaded hearing-aid salesmen well-up with tears of joy. The Noma Christmas lights over the mostly empty dance floor blinked indifferently to the rhythm of "She's Acting Single, I'm Drinking Doubles." One older couple, doing a sort of syncopated stagger, seemed to me either very uncoordinated or else very intoxicated.

Of course, as luck would have it, our entrance to the Why Not club exactly coincided with the end of the Gary Stewart song. Thus, our arrival was heralded with an uncomfortable silence. It was one of those silences where you hear nothing but a couple of clinking glasses and people clearing their throats. And judging from the looks we were getting, I figured the next thing I would be hearing was the sound of a firearm being cocked.

Even the old drunk couple over on the six-by-six dance floor had stopped their standing free-fall and seemed to be staring at us out of their stupor.

Under his breath, Altee Purvis whispered at me fearfully, "Remember all them snakes you run out that day?"

"Yeah," I said, my eyes darting back and forth from the drunk couple to the big shadows back by the pool table.

"You may have to help me out with a few more of 'em."

Let's hope not," I said.

"You ain't by chance still got that big iron bar we used to open them boxcars, do you?"

"Afraid not," I said, really meaning the "afraid" part with every ounce of my being.

Thankfully, as if guided by the very hand of God himself, the jukebox kicked back in at the Why Not club.

The song was

"Is Anybody Going To San Antone?"
by Charley Pride.

And I have to tell you, I'd always liked Charley Pride, but never more than at that particular moment. The highly pregnant pause which his song ended had me ready to mow, edge, and trim the shrubbery in his yard for life if he'd wanted me to. Heck, I would've even installed rockwool insulation in his house barehanded to bring it up to Department of Energy recommended levels. Charley Pride was my best friend at that moment.

And in a way, it seemed to somehow flip a switch in all the heads of all those people who'd been staring at us when we walked in. It was almost as if the song had made them think, "Oh yeah, that's a black guy singing that song, so maybe it's no big deal if another black guy comes in here and drinks beer with the rest of us."

And that's exactly what we did. I went about my duties as "the DJ from that country radio station" as usual, and Altee made a substantial cash sum from playing and winning pool against some newfound friends. Most notably, the two guys who'd been writing their names out in the parking lot earlier that evening.

He told everybody he was a rodeo rider who rode a lot out of Manor Downs and that his great-grandfather had been a buffalo soldier out in West Texas in the frontier days.

I just kept to myself and played music. Much of it music by Charley Pride, just to make sure our luck held out.

Two o'clock came pretty much without incident and we were out of there, much to my surprise. We drove back over to Altee's mom's house on the east side of Austin to have a couple of Old English 800s and relish our survival.

We sat out on the hood of my car, looked up at the stars, and jawed about this and that. The house he shared with his mother and two sisters was modest, but well-kept, and so I felt pretty much at ease.

He went inside to grab a couple more beers while I sat out on the car laughing to myself at the night's events. My head was laying up against the windshield, my legs comfortably crossed, when all of a sudden an arm came across my neck. A large-bladed knife glimmered in the moonlight scant inches from my face.

My first impulse had been to start laughing at Altee and his lame attempt to scare the hell out of me—until I realized it wasn't Altee at all.

The unfamiliar black face looked at me malevolently from beneath a black baseball cap.

"What you doin' over here white boy?" the face said, its eyes promising if they didn't like my answer they'd feel no remorse using the knife.

"I'm waiting on my buddy," I said, trying very hard to keep all bodily functions in check.

"Casper, you ain't got no buddies around here," he replied.

At the moment, I couldn't disagree with him, and cared little to get into a debate over that fact.

A car pulled up behind my new acquaintance and two more, equally as menacing figures got out.

"We gon' waste yo' white ass, what you think 'bout that?"

I didn't think he was really all that interested in an answer, so I didn't offer my opinion of the plan. Instead, I just thought how funny it was that I'd worried about Altee igniting violence over at the Why Not club, and here I was about to get filleted by some black guy who seemed less than interested in a dialogue between the races.

I was suddenly very conscious of how little cash I had in my wallet and tried to gauge just how active his knife hand might get when he discovered that fact and tried to work through his disappointment. Trouble was, he hadn't even asked for my wallet; or my car, for that matter. Apparently, they just wanted to mess somebody up, and I was available.

I thought about Altee and the first day on the job, and the squirming pile of snakes I got rid of for him. I thought about that big iron stake we used to open up the boxcars and just how handy that would come in about now.

Then I had the worst thought of all. The one that said Altee had sure been gone an awful long time for those beers. The one that said maybe he was part of all this. The one that said maybe there wasn't anybody to help me with this squirming pile of snakes.

I can truly say, without any doubt, that realization brought about the loneliest feeling I have ever had at any time in my life. A life which seemed about to come to an entirely premature end.

I'd trusted and even liked that black scumbag. I'd actually even worried about him. And this was what I'd gotten in return.

Maybe all the things I'd heard and always thought of as ignorant prejudice were really true after all. Maybe those arguments I'd gotten into with aunts and uncles and storekeepers and everybody else that it was wrong to treat black people differently really *had* been stupid and naive. This knife-wielding maniac with twelve hours worth of convenience store malt liquor on his breath sure made a good case for that anyway.

Helluva way to get done in, I thought, not knowing whether or not said thought would be my last.

The shot that exploded just a few feet behind my head sent me instinctively down to the hood of the car. I marveled at the lack of pain, other than the ringing in my ears from the noise, and waited to feel the warmth of the blood pouring out. I wondered if my mother would tell everyone she'd begged me to come home for the summer. I wondered if people would surmise I'd been trying to buy drugs or something. I wondered what the preacher would say about me.

More shots rang out as I rolled off the car trying to look dead and therefore unworthy of more lead. I guess I'd closed my eyes when the first shot had gone off and only worked up the courage to open them again from my new position on the grass next to my car.

It was Altee doing the shooting. His pistol was aimed just above the heads of the four or five oversized malt-liquor receptacles who'd just been showing me the versatility of their ginsu knives. They'd scattered in as many directions as their number and a car had squealed its tires somewhere off in the shadows. Other shots, which I assumed to be return fire from the visitors, ripped through the trees above our heads and echoed into the night.

"Friends of yours?" I asked, having trouble even hearing myself over the ringing in my ears.

"Used to be," Altee said.

"Thanks, man," was about all I could muster at the moment.

"That's cool," he returned nonchalantly. "You help me wit my snakes, I help you wit yours."

I wondered if the wet spot on my jeans originated from the early morning dew already on the grass, or from me.

After that, we continued to make our periodic trips together out to the Why Not club. While I did my deejaying duties, he continued to collect large sums of money from the other patrons, honing his billiard skills, which grew more formidable as the summer wore on.

Our truck loading and boxcar unloading prowess seemed to get better, as well.

The snakes underneath the fiberglass bales never did come back, but the evening ritual of going down to the Zip-in for cold liquid refreshment continued.

And, although he tried, Altee never could get me interested in going back to his neighborhood. Even in the daylight, I'd have no part of it.

Altee seemed a little embarrassed by the whole thing, as was I, so we avoided talking about it afterwards. Kinda like I didn't bring up anything about that little incident where I'd helped him out on our first day of work. At least, I didn't bring it up in front of other people.

Although it hadn't been true, he, I'm certain, felt as if I'd somehow saved his life. I was pretty well convinced he had, in fact, saved mine.

You probably wouldn't think so, but the whole thing put some kind of distance between us that hadn't been there before. I think he just felt bad about it all.

He never would say how well he knew those guys who'd come after me that night, or whether he'd had any trouble since. Just said the whole thing was stupid and left it at that. For my part, I felt bad about having—for a moment or two—suspected him of setting me up. I never told him that, but it did gnaw on me quite a bit. Especially the way things ended up.

Thankfully, the loading-dock beer chats we continued to have never ever turned to that evening the rest of the time we worked together. Then again, the rest of the time we worked together wasn't that much longer. A couple months at best.

One night, in the first part of September, I showed up and Altee didn't. He didn't call either.

After a couple of days of this, our usually absentee boss showed up to say he'd hired somebody else. He asked where he could find Altee to give him his final check. I had no idea, and said as much. Altee's mother didn't have a phone. I knew of no way to reach him, short of going over there. And I certainly had no intention of doing that.

The boss said he figured if he wanted it badly enough, he'd show up and get it.

"Other 'an that, Altee's fired and I ain't gonna lose any sleep over his black butt," was how he ended the conversation on the matter, adding that my new partner would be in tomorrow.

I don't know if it was some sort of quota thing, or just happenstance, but a new guy did show up the next day, and he, too, was black. A little older than me, maybe, and not nearly as talkative as Altee had been.

He seemed not to want to talk to me, so I left him to his own devices and didn't bother to invite him to join in on my nightly break and trip to the Zip-in store, which I continued solo.

Altee never did come back, at least not that summer.

I finally got tired of itching and digging little fiberglass needles out of my arms. I gave the Taggert Insulation Company notice in October. My new partner didn't seem to care much, nor did the management for that matter.

The summer of 1981 faded away over the next few months. Far more quickly, I might add, than the fiberglass remnants that were imbedded in my skin for at least the next couple of years.

I made several attempts to locate Altee over the next few years, but nothing ever came of any of it. And even if it had, I don't know if we'd have had anything to talk about. It's like they say, when you're looking for something, you're not going to find it.

Over time, I forgot Altee and the Taggert Insulation Company. That is, until the fall of 1989 when I began restoring an old house. Among the myriad things that needed attention in the old place was the insulation, or more accurately, the lack of insulation in the walls and ceilings.

Not really knowing anybody in that line of work, I exhumed the now eight-year-old memory of my itchy, snake-infested summer at the Taggert Insulation warehouse, and decided to give them a call if they were still in business. Having hired two guys like me and Altee, I had sincere doubts about whether they were.

A couple of fellows came out and gave the appropriate estimates. I also got estimates from a couple of other places, but found Taggert to be the low bid. On the appointed morning, two trucks arrived. They were truck numbers fifty-four and seventy-three, two that I could swear I had loaded more times than I cared to remember. Phantom fibergalss stung my arms as if to confirm the fact.

While the four guys in the truck unloaded the Owens-Corning, I easily resisted any temptation to offer them a friendly hand, jumping in the car and heading out to run some errands.

It was my sincere hope that the work would be done by the time I returned at the end of the day, as even the faint smell of fiberglass still made me borderline nauseous. I did start thinking again about the fun Altee and I had together, but finally figured it just as well that I didn't know what had become of him.

I pulled back into the driveway around sunset, pleased to find the trucks gone, the work completed. As I got to the front door, I found the bill taped next to the house numbers. I took it down and gave it a look. Handwritten underneath the computer generated numbers was a line that read, "No charge, per Mr. Purvis."

Just underneath that was another scribbled line that read, "P.S. Altee also requests that you stop by warehouse to help him get rid of a couple snakes. Old English 800s will be provided."

I hopped in the car and headed out.

As I pulled up to the warehouse and approached the black man sitting on the dock, I began wondering what the hell I was doing there, not to mention how the hell he bought this place. After the better part of ten years, we might well not have one damn thing to say to one another, but on I went, the brown paper bag with six-pack sitting next to him and the shaking head with wide smile growing more clear. As I passed the Porta-Can out in the parking lot, the laughing became audible. A constant, wheezing chuckle accented with the shaking of his head.

It was catching.

I was laughing, too, by the time I threw myself up on the dock and opened a can of that nastiness I still didn't quite have the stomach for. We laughed for the better part of a half an hour. Laughing and not really knowing why, but laughing nonetheless. Taking it all in. Thinking about the times before, the times in between, and now.

It was funny, if nothing else, the way things worked out. And I wanted to find out if we had anything left to talk about. I suppose he did, too. He started at it again like we'd never left the dock.

"You still wearing them damn cowboy boots."

"Yeah, but you're still in this damn insulation business," I came back. "And still drinking this damn paint thinner."

This being a Saturday, there were no poor, modern-day fools loading trucks like we'd done eight years before, and so we sat for a good four hours doing the appropriate recapping of the time since we'd last sat there.

I'd since gone into the advertising business as a copywriter, which is a nice name for someone who gets paid a lot of money for writing ads until they get their first novel published. He'd left Austin and gone into the used car business with a cousin in Houston. Business had been pretty good, but he had wanted to come back to Austin.

On a wild hair, he'd come back one weekend and made an offer to buy the place he'd gotten fired from years ago and, to his amazement, they'd accepted. Now he was making money hand over fist off the Austin building boom and living in a big place up on Cat Mountain, west of town. His old Chevelle had been replaced by a Mercedes-Benz. I suddenly understood why he'd been laughing.

I would be too.

Come to think of it, I was.

And it wasn't even my Mercedes.

"You know, I felt bad in a way, cause I never did say thanks," he threw out after another silence.

"For what?" I said.

"For not being white."

"You better have your eyes checked," I said.

"No, I mean, when we got to running together, you was just you. Not trying to talk like a brother when you was around me like a lotta white boys do, just being your old country-ass self.

I think that was the first time I ever thought a white person was all right."

"Well, I think you were probably the first black person I ever thought was all right," I said. "Of course, I didn't ever really know any before that."

An Old English 800 can came flying my way at that point, and the laughing started again.

There are friendships that are strong because of common backgrounds and interests, and there are those that are even stronger when you can appreciate your differences. After all this time we were just now examining this phenomenon for what it was.

The closeness of working together in a crummy place and then the distance time had put between us had all worked to help us both appreciate what it had been and want to at least have a chance to put an epitaph on the thing and eulogize its high points, if nothing else.

Now we'd done that and were glad for having made it so.

And it brings me no small amount of pleasure that we continue to meet once a month or so on the same loading dock in the evening to have a couple beers, laugh, and keep up with each other's families and foibles and hopes.

Probably won't solve any of the major problems that are still out there when we leave.

But we're two people talking *to* rather than *at* each other. And that, in and of itself, is a good thing.

After all, there are still plenty of snakes to kill out there.

"I'm going to Texas," my grandmother said. "You can stay here with your friends and your dance hall and the liquor and gun play if you've the mind to, but me and the babies are leaving right now."

Of course, she wasn't a grandmother at the time she said it. Matter of fact, she hadn't been a mother more than two or three years. It was the early 1930s, and she had just dropped the proverbial gauntlet to my grandfather.

Of course, he wasn't the grandfather I'd later know either; just some gangly, thirty-something-year-old with big ears, standing there out in front of the dance hall, not knowing what to do next.

Mom, as we all call my grandmother, had taken all she was going to take of his latest entrepreneurial venture and had thus decided to take matters into her own hands. That included driving the old Ford—for which she was not licensed—right on out of the town of Smackover and all the way to the East Texas oil fields that very night. Never mind that she possessed only a cursory knowledge of the vehicle's operation; departure time was at hand.

It was, as insurance companies and touchy-feely psychology types would say, a major life event. One that would shape a whole lot of people way beyond the two standing out there in that sweaty Arkansas night. Of course, they had no way of knowing that.

Mom just wanted out of a life that showed little promise of anything much beyond what she was now experiencing. A couple of newspaper stories, and talk among friends, offered hope of something better to the west of this place she'd always known. And if getting there meant learning how to drive a car and causing a bit of a disturbance out in front of this den of sin, so be it.

After all, disturbances were nothing new. Not to this place, anyway. In fact, the crack of sidearms' fire had recently become an almost nightly occurrence here, as locals blew off steam, got liquored up, and turned arguments into brawls.

This in itself was bad enough, but the house my grandfather had secured for my grandmother and their kids was located right next door. And that made the situation intolerable.

To his credit, my grandfather, or Papau as he would later be known to me, was only trying to find something to support his family. Decent jobs in 1930s Arkansas were scarce. Bars and dance halls were a relatively sure bet during this era of Prohibition, especially in an area that offered little beyond hard work, low pay, and even lower expectations for anything better.

Of course, I have to believe his venture wasn't totally of an altruistic nature, as I'm led to understand he did have some good measure of fondness for the night life in his earlier days. This is a trait I'd have never suspected. In his life as my grandfather, he spent his time teaching Sunday school classes at the Baptist church and reading constantly from a dog-eared, black leatherette-covered King James Bible.

That was all far in the future on this particular night in Arkansas, and for now young Dewey Warnix had to decide whether his young bride was bluffing or really intended to climb into that machine with the children and head off to some strange place called Texas.

The chirping of the crickets and strange little frog noises from off in the woods, along with the occasional strains of the music wafting out from the dance hall, were the only sounds to be heard.

My grandfather was thinking.

Trouble was, my grandmother had already thought it all out for him. This was made doubly apparent as she climbed into the car—into which the babies already had been placed— and, much to his surprise, managed to get the coughing beast to start.

For the briefest moment, he listened as the fiddles and occasional hoots and hollers from inside invited him to join them. Then one of the babies started crying and my grandmother kicked the car into gear and started rolling. She had his attention. Papau ran after the car and climbed in.

And although there were rough spots here and there, mostly relating to the shifting of gears and clutch operation, my grandmother actually was able to drive the old Ford pretty well. In any case, she certainly had no intention of turning the driving chores over to my grandfather, thinking he might try to pull a fast one and somehow or another work his way on back toward Smackover.

She drove through the night, keeping the car pointed pretty much west and a little to the south, stopping only when absolutely necessary.

One of those necessary occasions was at the behest of a Texas state trooper, shortly after they unceremoniously crossed the border at Texarkana. The red light mounted on the side of the shiny black and white roadster with a big lone star painted on the door glimmered off the pine trees and the faded paint of my grandparents' old beat-up Ford.

"I knew this was a fool idea," Papau said under his breath.

My grandmother just gave him the sharp end of her elbow and told him not to smart-off to the law man when he got up to the car window. Secretly, she wondered if the Texans had put up some kind of blockade to stop the flow of people out of Arkansas and whether they'd be put in jail, or worse, sent back home.

Texans were funny like that, she'd heard. They thought of themselves not so much as members of the United States, as they did an independent country which had blessed the rest of the Union with its grudging presence. Would-be immigrants from other places, especially places like Arkansas, were looked upon less than favorably.

Maybe it had something to do with the Alamo. But to my grandmother, it made little sense that these people would derive so much pride from an event where they'd been soundly routed by the Mexicans. Whatever the root cause, Texan pride was legendary amongst the people in Arkansas, and the thought of it was unsettling to her, especially as the knee-booted, Stetson-clad ranger made his way ever so slowly along the side of their old car.

He paused to shine his flashlight at the Arkansas tag, then continued, his boots crunching loudly in the gravel that covered the shoulder of the road.

"Good evening," he said, with the expected Texas drawl.

"Where y'all headed this time of night?"

"Texas," my grandmother blurted out, without really thinking about it.

"Well, you've certainly accomplished that much, I suppose," he replied.

My grandmother couldn't keep herself from looking at the hat. It was a big, fine-looking Stetson with a flat brim perched above a youthful, clean-shaven face. His white, starched shirt had fine, pointed collars, buttoned to the top; his pants, khaki, were held up by a leather pistol belt; and the western-style riding boots at the bottom of it all only added to the intimidating effect.

"Any particular place in our fine part of the world y'all might be heading toward?" he asked.

My grandmother, now thinking her first answer silly, replied, "Anywhere there's honest wages to be had, most probably the oil fields."

"I see," he said. "Well, the reason I stopped you is the fact you've no lights on the back of your automobile. Now, I can't speak for how such things are handled in Arkansas, but here, we much prefer that you have them if you're going to be motoring after sunset."

At this point, my grandfather started to chime in, spurred on by the way the lawman seemed to be talking down his nose about Arkansas, but his words were once again silenced by my grandmother's elbow.

"Well, we certainly didn't mean to cross any law," grandmother said, offering her best church-greeting smile to the Texas lawman.

"Could I please see your driving license?" asked the officer.

My grandmother got that funny feeling in the stomach we've all experienced at one time or another, and my grandfather got it too, only more potently.

It was then that my aunt, although still an infant, made her first significant contribution to the family; she threw a hideous bawling fit. All eyes immediately turned her way, most notably those of the Texas peace officer, whose heart began a rather steep ascent up the pity meter for these poor people he'd stumbled upon that night.

In no time, he was asking what that pretty little lady's name was and commenting on her lovely blonde locks. One thing led to another, and before long photographs of his own little pride and joy were out and being offered up to the would-be immigrants with the malfunctioning tail lights.

Directly, the whole question of driving licenses and the intentions of the occupants of this old beat-up Ford from Arkansas were lost, replaced by a common bond shared even between Texans and Arkansans—most notably, children and the raising and caring for same.

Empathy took the place of suspicion, and the lawman ended up escorting my grandparents and their infant children into the next town and over to the local motor court.

He laid down the cash for a night's stay, offered hope for the good Lord's blessings, and made his way back into the darkness, starched shirt, Stetson, pistol belt, boots, and all.

Taking charity was something generally frowned upon by my grandmother, as it was by most people, no matter how poor they were, but in light of her lack of a driver's license, she wisely determined to make an exception in this case. After all, she didn't want to wind up in some detention camp full of other Arkansan refugees awaiting deportation, though she had the sneaking suspicion such an occurrence would not bother my grandfather in the least bit.

To her way of thinking she'd already won half the battle; she'd gotten him across the state line. And now that they were over half way to their destination, she was more at ease with an uncertain future than she was with a more predictable past. She drifted off to sleep a little past 3:00 a.m., her last conscious thoughts the drunken shooting of pistols into the air that was no doubt going on somewhere back in Smackover. She wondered if my grandfather really believed she would've left without him.

His rhythmic snoring offered her no clues.

She wouldn't have left without him. Then again, she figured that was something she'd keep to herself, just the same.

Morning found them back on the road, just after eight o'clock, and an hour later, the would-be immigrants saw their equivalent of the Statue of Liberty.

What they saw were the oil derricks. Hundreds of them, sprouting rustily from among the tall pine trees. There were no plaques of welcome on them, offering invitation to poor, huddled masses, but they were welcoming nonetheless. At least they were to my grandmother.

My grandfather eyed them much more suspiciously, seeing only a lot of sweat and a good deal less fun in their operation than in the managing of a roadhouse. But he certainly had no fear of hard work; he'd done plenty of it, and if this was what was required to keep his wife and kids aside him, then so be it. The shock of leaving so quickly would wear off soon enough.

Stops at one place, then another, were made that day. Inquiries about work inevitably leading a little further on down the road, until, at last, they reached a place called Greggton.

It was there my grandfather found work with the Shell Exploration Company and temporary housing was provided in the form of a large tent. That would service them more or less well, except when the summertime afternoon downpours revealed a few leaks.

Eventually, an old shotgun-style house was secured a few miles out of town at a place called Seven Pines. On a road, ironically enough, that led back up to Arkansas. But any ideas my grandfather might have had about someday making use of it soon faded away as his new job proved steady and offered long-sought security. The only shots to be heard were the occasional blasts from my grandfather's rifle at a squirrel or rabbit for the dinner pot. The sum total of his night life consisted of playing with the kids and listening to the radio. There was sometimes music to listen to, reminding him of his dance hall days, but without the inherent dangers. His grudgingly abandoned get-rich-quick scheme was a lifetime away.

More kids came along. In fact, a lot more came along. Eventually, there were eight. Some survived to adulthood, while others succumbed to childhood disease. One was lost to a hunting accident in his teens.

And in spite of the hardships inherent in raising a large family, and the Depression that made it that much more difficult, my grandfather and grandmother faired well. After a time, they bought a large house in town and went into the real estate business as partners.

Though they never became wealthy, they never again had need for charity such as was offered by the Texas highway patrolman that first night.

I suppose you could say my grandmother's spur of the moment decision turned out to be a good one. I'd certainly say that, since her eternally uncalled bluff resulted eventually in my being born in this place instead of Arkansas. And in light of some of the more notable people who've recently come out of that state and into the public eye, that is something for which I'm quite thankful. Which is not to say there aren't some fine people there. A good number of relatives through my grandmother's side of the family live there still, and are as fine and colorful a group as you would ever want to meet.

None of them ever inhaled, either.

As for me, I'm glad my grandfather never called her bluff and instead went along for the ride. You can call it simple happenstance based on economics and the desire for something better, but I still like to believe a more divine hand was at play here. And while it may be on the self-important side to think all this transpired so as to position the place of my birth well to the west of that dilapidated dance hall in Smackover, it is a bit of poetic license that suits me, nonetheless.

My grandmother's impulsive move was the improbable beginning of my Texaness, the thing that set the wheels in motion to place me here. And in the end that is all that matters. The fact that it happened. And whether it was divinely scripted or just coincidence, I realize is of no importance, but it is fun to think about.

Somewhere way back in my ancestry are some Scots and Germans who made similar decisions to pack it in for better lives, and I suppose they, too, should be offered thanks for their lack of timidity. After all, they had to cross more than just a state line and a couple of bad potholes to follow their dreams, so I suppose their deeds were far greater than my grandmother's. But I never knew them.

Their paths, like those of others somewhat poor, are not well-marked. Their stories have faded into the depths, along with millions of other similar stories—noble, but not properly preserved.

But I do know my grandparents' story and how they came to be here. It is a story I can tell with some degree of authenticity. Most importantly, I have the opportunity to thank them.

Thanks to my grandfather for deciding to go along with the whole thing, however grudgingly.

And thanks to my grandmother for taking matters into her own hands at a time when ladies didn't generally do such things.

The young girl with the crying infant who made that decision so many years ago now looks back on that night from the perspective of one who has lived ninety-five years. And in spite of all the second-guessing that accompanies a long life, she still thinks she made the right decision.

For what it's worth, I concur, and I'm proud to be able to tell her so now. After all, it made a better life for her, and a native Texan of me.

In light of all the good that came from one girl's courageous decision, I suppose we could overlook the fact she never did bother to get that driver's license.

I won't tell if you won't.

OTTO LEE HEWITT

Otto Lee Hewitt used to mow the yard for the people across the road. He was a heavyset man who always wore a pair of Big Smith denim overalls with a big straw hat to keep his balding head from getting sunburned.

He had the funniest laugh I think I had ever heard at the young age of seven, and seemed to me so much more like us kids than most men of his age, which was forty-five or fifty at the time. My parents told me this was because he was mentally retarded—or simpleminded, as some of the older people referred to it.

The meaning was lost on me; all I knew was that he was fun to be around and always seemed to be happy and took the time to talk to us kids. He had the most infectious laugh I've ever heard and wasn't afraid to use it.

I can still remember playing football in the front yard once while he was pulling weeds. I ran head-on into a post oak tree. He laughed wildly until he saw I'd busted my head pretty good and was crying, whereupon, he ran over and carried me into our neighbors' house. By that time, he was crying as loudly as I was, all the time apologizing profusely for laughing at my misfortune.

Though I occasionally saw Otto Lee during my teens, I never again talked to him. As I passed his place, I sometimes got a glimpse of him plowing his little piece of land behind a mule in the old way and looking as happy as ever in spite of the hot labor in which he was engaged.

I always regretted not stopping and talking to him, but never more than just a few weeks ago when I got word Otto Lee had died. His nephew tracked me down through my parents and told me. He said Otto Lee had requested that I be one of the pallbearers at his funeral.

It was held at a small Baptist church outside of town, the hymns were sung a cappella, and the ceremony itself was simple. I took my place at the front left of the coffin and lowered it into the earth underneath a large pecan tree out behind his old place.

I cried without shame as his old straw hat was placed atop the coffin and the dirt was thrown onto it.

I glanced at the headstone that had already been placed there. It said "God bless Otto Lee, whose wonderful laugh now brings joy to the ears of the angels up above."

I walked out onto the recently plowed ground behind his old clapboard house and watched his mule grazing in the afternoon heat, blissfully unaware of the fate of his master.

THE LEGEND OF HANK'S EXTENDED HAIRCUT

Hank's Cherokee Lounge is one of the last vestiges of that great Texas institution known, quite unassumingly, as the beer joint.

It is a place that cares to be nothing more or less than what it is. That being an off-green frame building with a screen door that announces the arrival or departure of each guest, and one window with black paint across its top half and a Fedders window air conditioner underneath.

The sign out front is mostly lighted. In addition to spelling out the name of the place, it cheerfully announces that "Pearl Light Outshines Them All." The five bullet holes in the sign just serve to make the place look a good measure rougher than it really is.

It is a place our mothers told us to stay away from when we were younger and thus a place we were naturally drawn to when we got older.

Physical descriptions aside, probably the best way to convey what Hank's Cherokee Lounge is like is to relate one of the more legendary altercations between owner Hank and his wife, Mary. The latter is never *not* behind the bar, performing more or less simultaneously as both bartendress and un-quenchable patron.

One summer night, at the height of the evening business, Hank walked in after approximately two and a half weeks of extended R and R during which nobody, including Mary, had any idea where he was. Characteristically, he sat down at the bar behind which Mary toiled, lit up a Vantage 100 from the hard pack and, certainly not for the first time, he became the focus of one of Mary's more arctic glares.

Knowing he was there, but refusing to acknowledge him while serving drinks, Mary took care of those in line, then walked over to the 1964 Rock-Ola juke box, and in a manner that comes only from the rather curious combination of true skill and blissful drunkenness, kicked it out away from the wall with her left foot and knocked the plug out of the socket with her right.

David Allan Coe's rendition of "You Don't Ever Call Me Darlin', Darlin'" growled to a creaking halt, yielding near total silence and center stage to Mary, who, just to ensure it would continue that way, cracked a pool cue across the billiard table most convenient.

Hank, a man of fifty or so, who continues to slick back his silver hair in the style of the young George Jones, seemed not at all bothered by the rapid deterioration of his barroom's normally genial atmosphere.

He shifted slightly on his perch, the only sign of nervousness a tendency to tuck and re-tuck his Panhandle Slim western shirt, which had the annoying habit of riding up over his not-so-Panhandle-Slim belly.

Hank was a man of few words, but Mary clearly intended that tonight he would talk. The slur in her speech and recurring need to steady her five foot-two, ninety-three-pound frame against the pool table notwithstanding, Mary would not be dissuaded from her objective. Every patron in the place would attest to that, especially in light of the now-splintered pool cue swinging from her left hand.

"Where the hell've you been Mister Horse's Ass?" she barked, her large, brown-dyed hairdo moving in concert with her jaw, a living monument to the more than several cans of White Rain hair spray that had given their lives in its construction.

"I been running this damned hell-hole for three weeks, without any clue as to whether you'd run off with some strip dancer or were just layin' on the side of the road dead somewhere. And now you walk in here and park your blubber-butted self on your little leatherette throne and expect everthing to be just like it was? I don't think so. I wanna know where in high hell you've been and I wanna know now, Mr. Horse's Ass."

She seemed somehow more pleased with the sound of that name than most of the others she'd used on him in the past.

The forty or so stunned patrons of Hank's Cherokee Lounge sat, for the most part, looking at each other. A couple of those near the screen door tried to inch out along the wall like someone trying to avoid attention from a sniper. Some crawled under the many tables back towards the restroom. A few others just kept on drinking their beer and eating peanuts, treating her performance like an afternoon episode of All My Kids.

Hank, for his part, seemed almost unaware that the afore-mentioned verbal howitzers were even directed his way. Some acquaintances had speculated he was hard of hearing on one side, although others insinuated this was an affliction of convenience, recurring only during these rather frequent skir-mishes with his beloved bride and business partner.

As if to insure he had, in fact, heard it, Mary laid the question out again and punctuated it with a javelin-style toss of the busted pool cue into the abdomen of the bikini-clad girl on the Budweiser poster—the one that hung next to the autographed picture of Billy Martin.

The pained sighs of some of those in the unwilling audience were not so much out of surprise at Mary's violence as they were in mourning for the loss of an especially treasured piece of barroom landscape. There was, however, some small con-solation in the fact that she'd at least missed Billy; otherwise, it was widely thought that she'd be really mad now.

As it was, she was still waiting for an answer. So, for that matter, was everybody else. Some genuinely wanted to know where he'd been all this time, while others just wished to be done with the whole damned thing so the juke box could be turned back on.

As everybody sat listening, and Mary stood wobbling, Hank stubbed out his Vantage 100 from the hardpack and wheeled around on his stool 'til he was facing his wife. He sat there, surveying the audience she'd created and the general havoc she'd wrought thus far, noting that the bikini girl on the Budweiser poster was still smiling in spite of her injuries.

Billy Martin seemed indifferent.

Retucking his Panhandle Slim shirt yet again, Hank got up from his barstool and drew breath as if about to speak.

"Well? Where in the hell did you go?" Mary asked.

Her tone suggested this would be his last chance to answer this side of the I.C.U.

Hank lit another Vantage, took one eye-squinting puff and semi-mumbled his alibi.

"Had to go get a haircut."

Even if Mary wasn't, Hank seemed very pleased with that explanation. In fact, he almost grinned as he walked toward the screen door and repeated himself.

"Had to go get a haircut and now I'm goin' to the hardware store."

With that, he walked out of the screen door and let it bounce behind him.

Those left variously seated and standing back inside the barroom waited for Mary's reaction. Her wobbly gaze circled back around each of them, like the searchlight in one of those German prison camp movies.

Finally, somebody had the nerve to ask if they could get another pitcher.

"Hell, I imagine," she said.

The collective sigh of relief was almost tangible as she walked back towards the 1964 Rock-Ola and stuck the plug back in the wall.

David Allen Coe grunted back to life right at the part where he was drunk the day his mom got out of prison and he went to pick her up in the rain but she got runned over by a damned old train.

At this point, life at Hank's Cherokee Lounge returned pretty much to normal.

Although, to this day—some twelve years later—the broken pool cue remains lodged in the otherwise flawless abdomen of the bikini girl on the Budweiser poster.

And Hank still hasn't gotten back from the hardware store.

MODERN-DAY THINGS

AS SEEN THROUGH

DECIDEDLY UNMODERN EYES

———————

This old porch is just a long time waitin' and forgettin',
Rememberin' the coming-back and not cryin' about the leavin'.
And rememberin' the fallin' down and the laughter of the cursed luck,
From all those sonsabitches who said we'd never get back up.

Robert Earl Keen, Jr. and Lyle Lovett
"The Front Porch Song"

M y bank changed it's name the other day. Of course there's really nothing unusual about that. In this part of the country, it's like saying the sun came up again. In fact, I guess if you want to be truthful about it, the shocking news would be if a bank around here was to hang onto the same name for say, longer than the terms of their extremely low-interest-paying six-month CDs.

I know they've had a rough go of it in the last few years, but I, for one, would be perfectly content to just get hold of the amount of money they've spent on name changes and the inherent signage and printing costs that go along with said changes.

As an example, there's one bank in town that, once upon a time, was called RepublicBank. Well, things got kinda tough for them, so a few years back they merged with the First National Bank. After much travail, gnashing of corporate teeth, and, no doubt, a large fee to some naming consultant, they arrived at a new name. First RepublicBank.

Good call.

Well, probably due in part to the expense of finding that first new name, it wasn't long before this new bank got into trouble and had to be bought out by North Carolina National Bank. Probably in an effort to avoid the stigma of an out-of-state bank, they rather discretely and rather cleverly deigned that their new name here would be simply NCNB.

Down came the recently hung First Republic signs, up went the new NCNB signs.

Were you supposed to now call this place by its initials or was the new name meant to be pronounced "NucNub?"

I never knew for sure. But then again, it didn't matter, for quicker than you can say "Sorry, we can't loan you the money," that name, too, was relegated to the dust heap of doomed banking monikers.

Seems people had figured out that the NC in the name might well stand for North Carolina, thus making this an out-of-state bank. Back to the nom-de-banc drawing board.

This time, the new bank name was NationsBank, meant to indicate this was a totally new bank, a bank for all of us—especially those of us with short attention spans.

Well, as luck would have it, I recently found myself in need of a loan. I dreaded the thought of the paper work and accompanying tedium. In fact, I dreaded it so much, I sought to do anything to put the event off. Even to the point of pausing as I walked in the bank's door to look at the sign to see how many of the old names I could still see underneath the new painted one.

It was then that a surefire, foolproof way to secure a loan here occurred to me.

Being bankers, they'd want to know for sure that I was in a business that offered good potential for future profit, right? They'd want to know my market was solid, so they could be assured of getting their money and more back, right?

Thus it was that as I came to the blank on the loan application that asked about my employment, it was with only a small measure of guilt that I wrote . . .

". . . sign painter."

THE FUTURIST

The other day I had what I'd guess you'd call the good fortune to attend a speech by a guy who calls himself a "futurist." Now, I'd heard of economists, communists, and I even regularly see a dentist, but this was certainly my first experience with a futurist.

I'm not talking about the Ouija board-toting, Dionne Warwick's Psychic Friends Hotline kind of futurist. I'm talking about a guy who says he can take a look at what's going on now, and tell you what's probably gonna happen in the way of trends in the future.

I'd never known there was such a thing. And I found myself wondering what it is you study in school to become a futurist. As far as I know, you can't get a degree in it, not this side of a mail-order operation, anyway. And besides, even if there was a college degree program for futurists, it seems to me they'd have to wait a few years before conferring it, to make sure these future futurists had successfully learned what they'd been taught.

Well, by the time I got through considering all that, he was well into his presentation, and I must admit, he was pretty good. He was telling us we were living in the age of the victim ethic, where everybody's trying to make themselves out to be some kind of victim of something or other to get the spoils, or, in most cases, punitive court damages that go along with being said victim.

And I could agree with that. I mean, after all, the only thing you have to do to see that is look at the evening news. But I'm afraid that's about the spot where I parted ways with my futurist friend. You see, that's when he started talking about what the baby boomers are gonna do in the next few years, and what the "generation x'ers" are gonna do, and what we can expect from the "millenium generation." The millenium generation is that generation which has yet to be born, but has already been named by futurists. After all, they are futurists.

That's when I started wondering if there's a group of people who get paid to sit around and think up names for generations. It's also when I started thinking of the absurdity of trying to lump all people born in certain time frames into one monolithic group. Be it for futurist purposes or otherwise, it's absurd to think all those people are gonna do the same things just cause they were born with the same number on their paperwork.

I was born in 1960, which I guess puts me on the tail end of the baby boom generation. And I know lots of other people born in 1960 or thereabouts, and the year of birth is about all we have in common with each other. Some are rich, some are poor, some did post-graduate work, and some are drunks. Some are or have been all of the above at one time or another.

But none of them are quite the same. And none of their lives or my life have taken their little twists and turns in lockstep with one another, nor do I expect them to. After all, that's one of the things that makes this little ride we call life just a little more interesting. At least, that's what I always thought.

So, as he continued to go on about what it was we are all going to do in the next couple of decades, I guess I started to look at this fellow—who I think is a baby boomer—with somewhat of a jaundiced eye.

As for the guy sitting next to me, I don't know what he thought. For all I know, he might have believed what he was hearing. After all, he was a generation x'er, I think. And you know how they are.

Don't get me wrong though. I don't think there's anything wrong with someone going out on a limb and trying to predict what it is we as a society are all gonna do. And I guess there's probably even good money in it. But all things being equal, I guess I'd just as soon dig out the old Ouija board and leave it at that.

M rs. Mattie Williams finally ended her holdout a couple of weeks ago. It didn't have anything to do with guns or hostage situations or SWAT teams, so it didn't make much of a splash in the news. Truth is, she didn't give in voluntarily, but old age and the decision by relatives to put her in a nursing home ended the holdout for her.

For the last ten years or so, she'd refused dozens of multimillion dollar offers for her home and the couple of acres of land on which it sat on South Cooper Street in the town where I grew up. Others around her had seen fit to sell their land and be done with it. But she held on. In the end, her home of sixty or seventy-odd years was gradually surrounded by a huge shopping mall, strip centers, and chain restaurants on what had once been the sleepy little southern edge of town.

To most, it was an odd little juxtaposition, her neat, well-kept little clapboard house and attendant garden, with crepe myrtle and oak trees, surrounded by the encroaching icons of modern suburbia. The mall, which sat behind her, was called "The Parks," a less than truthful moniker for something mostly asphalt and concrete. Up and down the street across from her house were Bennigan's restaurants, a Sportstown, a Sam's Club, and the biggest abomination of all—something called a "Hypermart."

Still, Mattie Williams's little place stood there, like it always had, only now without the peaceful view.

Don't get me wrong, I'm no treehugger or loather of the free enterprise system or the development that inevitably goes with it. It's just that retailers seem to build nothing but huge warehouses that strip out all that was once there in favor of thousands of items at the lowest guaranteed prices, everyday. Complemented by oceans of asphalt parking lots so that the overweight masses who shop there won't have to let any exercise cloud their shopping bliss.

Little places like Mattie Williams's become just one more casualty, a part of the roadkill that accompanies such developments. And me, and maybe a half dozen or so other people, take notice of it all and lament.

When I saw the newspaper story about her family finally selling the land a couple of weeks ago, I drove out to there to take a look, not really sure of why I was doing it. By that time, the bulldozers had already done their work. The house was a pile of boards. The carcasses of the once-proud oaks and crepe myrtles lay twisted in another large heap nearby, the blooms of the crepe myrtles only now beginning to wither and die.

Out by the street was a hastily placed sign, cheerfully announcing the impending arrival of the theme restaurant that would soon occupy Mrs. Mattie Williams's former space on this earth. A restaurant. A "family" restaurant. No doubt just as boring and antiseptic as any of a thousand others cookie-cuttered out across the country.

As I stopped at the light to turn out onto South Cooper Street, I glanced back over my shoulder and took one last look at the barbed wire fence that still stood guard between Mattie Williams's world and what our world has become.

I guess some fences can only hold so long.

Ozone Alert

There's a new phenomenon in my little part of the world. It's called an ozone alert. Living here, I've gotten used to tornado watches and warnings and freeze warnings and the like, but I wasn't quite sure what to think when they started this ozone business.

When they issue these ozone alerts, they tell us that the problem is there's too much ozone in the air, and that that's a bad thing. We're not supposed to mow our yards or edge with our weedeaters, or get stuck in road construction delays with our cars. This is all fine and well and good. I'm as excited as the next fella to have a good excuse not to weedeat.

The real gripe I have with this whole ozone alert thing is this: they tell us the reason we have these things is that there's too much ozone in the air. Ozone put out by emissions from cars and things, and—I don't know—cows with gastrointestinal difficulties. But is it just me, or did Al Gore spend a lot of time lameting the ozone hole in the atmosphere during the most recent presidential elections? I seem to recall him saying we'd all better do something about fixing that hole in the ozone layer or we were going to turn into walking carcinomas.

And now they're telling me we're having an ozone alert because there's too much ozone around here? Seems to me, they should be asking me to work overtime with my weedeater, and spend more time stuck in traffic. I mean, they did say we have an ozone hole, didn't they? And we got your ozone right here. So what's the deal? Do they want ozone or do they not?

Now I hear our benevolent government, in the form of the EPA, has let it be known that if we don't get rid of all this ozone, we're going to have to take our cars to these special places where they'll charge us for the privilege of getting said cars blessed by them. For a large fee, of course.

Ahh, now it all makes sense.

There is, in fact, a hole we need to be worried it about, but it's not in the ozone layer. It's a big, black hole, far more ominous than any ozone hole, into which, I have a feeling, a whole lot more of my money is about to be sucked.

I n the spring of 1981, I had reached the point in my time at The University of Texas at Austin where I had some choices in the types of classes I could take to fulfill my English requirements. Those requirements for a journalism major were substantial, and I found myself in dire need of something beyond the usual composition classes.

The course catalogue, which in size resembled that of Sears and Roebuck, held little that excited me until I reached a small section of M-W-F classes entitled "The Literature of Texas and the Southwest."

No doubt some would find the very title to be an oxymoron, but I knew better. I determined then and there to sign up for it.

The reading list included *The Log of a Cowboy,* by Andy Adams, *The Raven,* which was the story of Sam Houston's life, *Giant,* and a book I'd never heard of called *Good-bye To A River,* by one John Graves.

Reading lists up to that point in my less-than-illustrious college career had held little sway in the use of my discretionary time, and just by looking at the titles, I greatly doubted any of that was about to change.

Fortunately, I opened Graves's book first. The premise of the book was simple enough. A man, who had grown up in Fort Worth and become infatuated with the beauty of the Brazos River west of town, had gone on a three-week canoe trip down the stream to take one last look.

The Corps of Engineers, in their own heavy-handed way, had decided to dam up this section of the river in its entirety, and Graves meant to have some final time with it to pay his respects and reflect on what it had meant to him. Along the way, he kept a journal and listened to what the silence of his old friend, the river, had to say.

Far from just a nature journal, the book wove a tale of the place and the people who had inhabited the area. It didn't seek to glorify the white settlers who had come there in the 1880s. Nor did it seek to bestow Sainthood on the Comanches, who had fought savagely to keep their territory. It simply presented them for what they were—human inhabitants of a land not entirely friendly to habitation—humans whose characteristics in battle and in peace reflected much that was good and much that was not.

So what began as merely a title on a reading assignment list became something much more than that. Mr. Graves's book opened my eyes to my heritage, the people who'd shaped who I was and who I would no doubt become. It confirmed for me that there were others who looked at this part of the world through a different filter than most—others who shared a disdain for the drive-thru convenient, rip-all-the-trees-out and put-up-a-shopping-mall kind of world in which we now lead our sanitary little lives.

But more than anything, Mr. Graves had that voice. The one I'd been looking for. The one that allowed me to take all the feelings I'd been carrying around all this time and trade them in for words.

And while the literature class didn't turn my college career around, I did, thereafter, find myself proselytising to all who would hear it, the virtues of *Goodbye To A River* and the rest of the man's works.

To my chagrin, however, Mr. Graves has written only four books that I know of, which leads me to conclude that, like gold, things literary are more precious when found in small amounts.

THOSE LITTLE BEARDS

I don't know, call me crazy, but it seems to me more and more, things that are supposed to be acts of rebellion or a confirmation of your individuality end up being just the opposite.

Last night, I'm flipping across the TV channels, when I catch of glimpse of Garth Brooks on some kind of special. Only this time, that silly looking little air-traffic controller-type headset microphone wasn't the only odd thing he was wearing.

He also had one of those little beards.

You know what I'm talking about—those little "artist beards," "beatnik beards" as my dad would say. Little beards that just surround your mouth and cover part of your chin and say "Hey, I'm my own man, wearing no other man's yoke. I'm no crowd follower, pretty-boy Ken doll. I'm a bohemian for crying out loud.

"I'm a don't wear Dockers, torn flannel shirt, pierced-body-part kinda guy. You can tell, because I've got one of these beards."

Only trouble is, so many guys have decided to make this statement of individuality, the real rugged individualists today are those who never bothered to grow this facial hair in the first place.

So, surely, many of those gravitated toward the beard thing will soon find themselves fleeing to some other statement of creativity and coolness. Maybe dark socks and wingtips with Bermuda shorts, or perhaps the occasional jumpsuit with an embroidered marlin across the front will become the next refuge of hip.

In the meantime, I'm supposed to meet this business associate of mine in that mecca of hipness, Los Angeles. This fellow is someone who I've only talked to over the phone. I've agreed to meet him at this trendy restaurant out there. Of course, having never seen me before, the guy wants to know how he'll recognize me.

I told him just to look for the only man without one of those little beards.

"Surely," he said incredulously, "there'll be more than one guy in the whole restaurant without one of those things."

I said, "Yeah, I suppose you're right. There'll probably be two of us without the beards. But I'll still be easy to spot.

"I'll be the one without the ponytail."

The body of the Mattress Giant was lying lifeless on the roof of the strip shopping center across the street. For the last several months, this inflatable man had stood proudly over the Mattress Giant Discount Sleep Superstore, right between the quick print place and the discount computer supercenter.

With one huge outstretched arm, he beckoned tirelessly at the traffic along the freeway, seeming to say, "Come on in and try out a couple of our box springs with perfect posture back support, and—heck—we'll throw in a futon for free."

I'd just come into my office Monday morning and there the Mattress Giant lay: on his back, left leg folded underneath him, eyes frozen open in a deathly trance, mouth agape.

He looked kinda like one of those dead soldier pictures in World War II-era *Life* magazines. Another victim of weekend violence, no doubt.

The Mattress Giant had been a polyethylene-looking fellow, about thirty feet tall, wearing a yellow shirt, blue cut-off knee pants, and sandals. The Mattress Giant seemed to me a hybrid of the Pillsbury Doughboy, Mr. Clean, and the

Michelin Man, all rolled into one aerial icon of shopping convenience.

Mattress Giant wanted nothing more than to be our friend. But now he was gone. And in the gray silence of a Monday morning, I tried to imagine how he might have met his end.

Had it been a Saturday night brawl turned ugly with the Kip's Big Boy from down the road? Or perhaps an old-fashioned showdown with the Waterbed Genie? Or had he maybe downed a little two much helium and in his exuberance tried to get amorous with a passing blimp?

Regardless of the cause, the Mattress Giant had gone to that year-end factory clearance sale up in the sky, the loud hissing of his escaping essence still audible throughout the neighborhood.

I was going to miss the Mattress Giant.

And I felt sorry for his family, too. Such a senseless loss.

Besides, where would the cops ever find a big enough piece of chalk to draw that funny outline around his body?

WITH MANY THANKS TO MRS. REEVES

They give out condoms in some public schools now. It's for the protection of the kids, so I'm told. They don't pray, though. That wouldn't be right.

I don't know, call me old-fashioned, but I'm troubled by these facts. I guess I should be happy they're at least giving the kids something. After all, one need only look at SAT scores to confirm that students might well be leaving school with little beyond that telltale circle indented on the outsides of their wallets.

The more I see of such stupidity, the more fortunate I feel to have been placed in the second grade class of Mrs. Sarah J. Reeves back in the fall of 1967. While all around the world was turning upside down, little ladies and gentlemen were being formed within the walls of her classroom.

Actually, little of the turmoil one so often associates with that time ever reached any of the neighborhoods around the W.R. Wimbish Elementary School. Young men who were drafted from that part of the world did their duty and went off to war. Those left at home supported them and waited hopefully for their return.

The turmoil the news anchors kept telling us about was nearly as far away as the war itself. Very few of the bad things happening in the country at the time ever found their way into our little part of the world. Certainly not into Mrs. Reeves's classroom.

Even the edicts of the Supreme Court held little sway around here. Although it had been five years since the Court's ruling which outlawed prayer in public schools, our classes began each morning with a brief blessing.

Looking back, I suppose this was my first experience with breaking the law. And in writing this, I'm assuming whatever statutes of limitations there might be with regard to this case have long since expired. Although I suppose if Mrs. Reeves were to be tried at this late date, she might be able to avoid any serious time by volunteering for community service. Perhaps she might be forced to distribute condoms in a local high school as repayment of her debt to society.

I shudder to think what sort of national scandal would have resulted had such a thing as praying occurred in more recent times. As for the students in her class, none of us grew up to become unscrupulous television evangelists. Nobody's parents called in the ACLU. And, as far as I know, not one of us was irrevocably damaged by the thought that there might be a God up there, overseeing our growing up.

Those little daily prayers did have an effect on me, though. They served to make me realize, even at that young age, that God was more than a Sunday school thing, and that thought should be given to Him, not just when report cards came out, but also in appreciation for the good things with which He had blessed us.

A few years back, I looked Mrs. Reeves up and called her to thank her for that. There was lot in the news at the time about the debate over prayer in public schools and I wondered if anyone had ever thanked her for the good she had done, in spite of modern society's crusade to end the reign of such evil, intolerant people as herself.

Her voice was as sweet as I remembered it, always enthusiastic and loving in praising us, and just as loving, but serious, when disciplining us—such as the time my friend Ross Brewster said "booger-snot" out loud during reading class.

Maybe we still had prayer in our classes because things change more slowly in Texas. Admittedly, this is not always a good thing. But at the risk of being labeled a flat-earther, or worse, I suggest that there are many things we've seen fit to do away with that we shouldn't have.

The things that Mrs. Reeves stood for are the very things most often mocked and made fun of today. Surprisingly, we look on in shock as the evening news relates the latest shooting or drug bust at school. As often as not, these stories are followed by the news of the ACLU's latest battle in court to protect our children from that most menacing threat of all—prayer.

In most places, that's not even an argument anymore. Only back here in Texas, and a few other "backwards" places, do some still battle the conventional wisdom on this matter. Meanwhile, in the public schools of New York and Los Angeles, the only exposure most students will ever get to such a threat is at the funerals of classmates.

Not coincidentally, most of those with the money to do so have taken their kids out of the public schools and whisked them off to safer environs. And I'll assume I am not the only one who finds no small irony that these safer environs often come in the form of parochial schools.

Maybe I'm just too backward-looking for my own good. Certainly, it wouldn't be the first time someone had accused me of this. And were you to call me politically incorrect, I would admit that it's so and thank you for saying as much. But at a time when what's right and what's wrong have been blurred by the new religion of relativism, maybe an occasional dose of—dare I say it—God, or the "G-word" if you prefer, wouldn't be such a bad idea.

As for me, I just thank God for people like Mrs. Reeves. Or am I allowed to do that anymore?